Beach Bar Blues

A Trials of Katrina Novel

Maureen P. Moore

Published by Northern Amusements, Inc., Windsor, Ontario.

This is a work of fiction. All the characters, organizations, and events portrayed in this novel are either products of the author's imagination or are used fictitiously.

Beach Bar Blues, Maureen P. Moore - 1st Edition
Trade Paperback
ISBN 978-1-0689823-4-7
e-Pub version
ISBN 978-1-0689823-5-4

This book and others by Northern Amusements are available in electronic format.
Visit our web site at www.northernamusements.com

Cover by Dale J. Moore
Edited by Maureen P. Moore / Dale J. Moore
Printed and bound in Canada and/or the United States.

DEDICATION

To Ralph, the perfect beach companion.

Table of Contents

1   PUB 'N GRUB - WHERE'S THE LOVE?

With The Great Upheaval in full swing, and Tate AWOL for the past week, Katrina decided to suck up her doubts and give him a call.

She knew she'd been acting like a bipolar whack job for the past month, but she just couldn't help herself. It was as if that damn psychic had put a hex on her. Tate finally told her to call him when she was normal again, when whoever had taken over her brain gave it back to her, when she no longer thought the sky was falling.

Katrina still thought the sky was falling, but she called Tate anyway. He sounded glad to hear from her. Tentative, but glad. She'd missed his voice. She'd missed his body. They made a date.

The Pub 'n Grub was still quiet when Katrina walked in, stomping snow off her boots and taking off her hat, praying she didn't have hat head. February in Toronto. At least two more months till spring. *Somebody shoot me,* thought Katrina.

She looked eagerly around for Tate, but he wasn't there yet. The place was pretty quiet – not yet time for the happy hour crowd. Katrina's best friend, Cathy, was behind the bar, as she usually was on Thursday nights – unless she had a play or rehearsals going on. Cathy worked at the Pub 'n Grub (or the

Grub, as all the regulars called it) a couple of times a week, though she didn't have to work. Her live-in boyfriend, Stewart, would've been happy to let her stay home and work on her acting, directing and playwriting. But Cathy insisted on being her own woman, and not dependent on a man. "Not totally, anyway," Cathy would giggle.

Katrina had left her salon, Kat's Kuts, early and in the hands of her feature stylist Kevin. And since Tate, who landscaped in the summer and did the odd cabinetry job in the winter, wasn't working, Katrina had figured they'd have the bar pretty much to themselves at this hour. Since the fight, neither one of their apartments seemed like a good idea. Neutral ground would be best.

And then she saw Heidi. Damn. Her friend was sitting elegantly at the bar sipping a cocktail.

Not good. Tate and Heidi were not big fans of each other. All Katrina needed was for them to get at each other's throats when all she wanted was some quiet time with Tate.

Katrina took a deep breath and walked over to greet her friends.

"Talk to Tate yet?" asked Cathy, wiping down the bar where Katrina slid onto a stool.

"No," said Katrina, shaking out her long blonde hair, wanting to brush it but not wanting to look too vain. "He's meeting me here any time now."

"Now that should be interesting," sneered Heidi, sipping on her cocktail.

"Margaritas?" said Katrina, ignoring the snide comment and sliding off her coat and hanging it on a hook on the bar by her knees. "What happened to your dirty martinis?"

"I'm off to Mexico tomorrow, silly," replied Heidi. "I've rubbed it in enough – how could you have forgotten?"

"The Great Upheaval," said Cathy, throwing down a cocktail napkin in front of Katrina. "That's all she's talked about for the last month."

"Good God," said Heidi, "we're not going to start talking about that psychic shit again, are we?"

"It's not shit," replied Katrina. "What if I really do meet a tall, dark handsome stranger? What do I do then?"

"Pray he's not like Jonathan," said Cathy. "Some Prince Charming he turned out to be."

Heidi raised an eyebrow. "I heard he had his moments before – "

"*Before*," cut in Katrina, "being the operative word. Can we please not talk about him?"

"Well, there was Jake," said Heidi, "if a cop is your idea of a good time."

"Not all men have to be a 'good time'," said Cathy. "There's more to life than – "

"Than being miserable," Heidi finished. "Why date someone who's going to make your life hell? Dating should be fun."

"If you call one-night-stands dating," said Cathy, "then you've done a lot of dating in your time."

Heidi laughed. "I seem to remember you 'dating' a couple of girls here and there, before you latched on to Stewart." She laughed again. "So who bought dinner on those 'dates', Cathy?"

Cathy snorted. "At least we were civilized enough to *have* dinner. At least we didn't just fall into bed after the first hello."

"Sometimes it's better not to talk," said Heidi.

"You should know," said Cathy.

"Anyway," said Heidi, tired of the subject and turning to Katrina, "Where is The Slug? I sure hope he hasn't changed his mind on you."

"What have you got against Tate anyway?" said Katrina, losing patience with all this bickering.

Heidi shrugged. "I just think you could use someone a little livelier."

"He's lively when he needs to be," snapped Katrina, making Heidi and Cathy stare; it wasn't like their sweet Katrina to be temperamental…well, it hadn't been till a month ago, anyway.

"Ooh-hoo," said Heidi. "Good comeback. But really, Katrina, you're so gorgeous; you could do so much better. Like someone rich, for instance."

"Katrina's not into money like you are," said Cathy.

"Well she should be," said Heidi. "She should have some guy taking her for fabulous dinners, Caribbean vacations, nights on the town…"

"GIRLS!" said Katrina, "You're giving me a headache. Do you have to bicker tonight? I'd almost swear you two were a couple, the way you go at it." She sighed. "Look, I admit things between Tate and me haven't been…great….lately, but he's meeting me here tonight so we can talk, and I'd appreciate a little – "

"What would you appreciate?" came a voice over Katrina's shoulder, and she looked up to see Tate standing beside her, snow nestled on his Maple Leafs toque and in his tousled blond hair. It had only been a week, but she'd missed him. Why did he look so much better than she'd remembered? Ridiculous – you'd think he'd just come back from the wars. Which, she supposed, he kind of had.

Crap, thought Katrina – how much had he heard? He certainly wouldn't appreciate her talking about him to her girlfriends – though men must be at least bright enough to know that happened all the time – they only had to watch any rom-com to know that. Though when she'd last seen a romantic comedy with Tate was beyond her. "Too much mushy talking about feelings," he always said, and clicked over to the Sports Network. Tate was easy-going about most things, but watching chick flicks wasn't one of them.

"I'd appreciate a drink," said Katrina quickly.

"Me too," said Tate. "Why's the bartender so slow?" He grinned at Cathy, who he liked, and ignored Heidi, who he didn't. He kissed Katrina lightly on the cheek with snow-dampened lips and slid onto the stool beside her.

Heidi smiled thinly at Tate, and Katrina was afraid she might blurt out something about The Great Upheaval, even though Katrina had sworn both her girlfriends to secrecy on the subject. But Heidi simply said, "We were talking about my little trip to Mexico tomorrow. I think your girlfriend's getting a little envious."

"Oh," said Tate, loathe to even talk to Heidi. "Who can blame her, with this weather." He turned to Cathy. "I'll take a pint of Blue. Kat?"

"Oh," said Katrina, realizing she was staring at Tate and reluctantly dragging her eyes away. She glanced over at Heidi's margarita. "I'll have one of those."

"You sure?" said Cathy, as she poured Tate's draft. "They're two and a half ounces, you know."

"I know what they are," snapped Katrina, suddenly irritated and not sure why.

Cathy gave her a look but passed Tate his beer and started on Katrina's cocktail.

Katrina, embarrassed by her rudeness, said, "I'd love to go to Mexico right this minute, too. But we have plans this weekend, don't we, Tate?"

"Plans?" said Tate innocently, wiping some foam from his upper lip. "What plans? The only plan I have is to go over to Rick's on Sunday and watch the game with a few of the guys."

Heidi and Cathy exchanged looks. They knew very well it was Katrina's birthday on Sunday – she'd mentioned it every time she talked about The Great Upheaval.

Cathy handed Katrina her margarita, and she downed it in two gulps. "Give me another one," she demanded, glaring at Tate.

Tate looked concerned. "Kat, are you really sure – "

"I'm sure," said Katrina, wiping salt off her lips. It stung. Like the way Tate's words had just stung.

Katrina was dying to mention her birthday, but she was damned if she'd remind Tate – she'd talked about it for the past month, suggesting different scenarios: a sleigh ride up north somewhere, a romantic overnight in a cosy inn, a special dinner.... But if Tate couldn't even remember all that...She sucked down her second margarita, seeing Heidi and Cathy out of the corner of her eye, both about to say something. She gave them a warning look as she turned away from Tate.

"Look," said Tate, lowering his voice as he sensed Heidi and Cathy trying to listen in, "We haven't seen each other in a week. Let's just have a couple of drinks and have some fun, hmm? You remember what that's like, don't you?" He tried to

11

make this sound cheery, but it came off as sarcastic. Katrina burped, ignored him, and ordered another margarita. Cathy looked worried, but Katrina glared at her and Cathy could see how distraught she was, so she made it.

Tate sighed. "You know you can't drink like that, Katrina."

"Sure I can," she said as she lurched against Heidi. Heidi, seeing Cathy making the margarita, ordered another one for herself as she pushed Katrina back into an upright position.

Tate squeezed Katrina's shoulder. "Let's say we go someplace quiet and talk? Huh? Why don't you come with me right now?"

"I'm not sure if I ever want to come with you again," said Katrina, and realizing what she'd said, suddenly started to giggle. The other girls caught it and laughed, too.

Tate shook his head in disgust and downed his beer, trying to maintain his temper. He was a very laid-back guy, but this was getting to be too much.

"Matter of fact," Katrina said, straightening with some effort, trying to look poised. "I think if I'm coming anywhere, I'm coming to Mexico with Heidi tomorrow."

"WHAT!?!" cried Heidi and Tate at the same time, both horrified.

"Well," said Katrina, "if *you* can't remember my birthday, I bet I can celebrate it in Mexico with somebody else."

Tate stared at her. "Don't be ridiculous. Is this all about your birthday shit again?" He spoke without thinking, before he could stop himself, and he saw the venom in Katrina's eyes.

"Birthday *shit*?!?" she cried in disbelief.

"Here we go," said Heidi with a giggle.

"It's not funny!" cried Katrina. "It's very important to me, and Tate should understand – "

"I understand you've been acting like a maniac for nearly a month," said Tate, "and you won't even tell me what's wrong." He looked angrily at Cathy and Heidi. "*They* probably know more than I do."

Cathy looked guilty and hurried over to a customer whose drink was still full. Heidi tossed her hair nonchalantly and peered around the bar. "If there was anyone in here worth talking to, I'd offer to leave you two alone. But there's not, and this is way too much fun."

"I thought we were here to talk," said Katrina, "not accuse each other of things."

"Shit," said Tate, "You're the one who hasn't been talking. All you've been doing is whining about your birthday and acting bonkers – for weeks." He stopped suddenly, thinking. "Christ, you're not pregnant, are you?!?" He grabbed for Katrina's drink, but she held it firm. Still, half of it sloshed onto the bar.

"Oh, seriously," said Katrina, dabbing at the spilt drink with her fingertips and licking it up.

"Well you're not, are you?" persisted Tate.

Heidi started laughing. "Pregnant! Now *that* would be hilarious!"

Katrina and Tate both glared at her, and she shrugged. "Just sayin'."

"No," said Katrina. "I am definitely not pregnant."

"Then what?" asked Tate, grabbing a napkin and wiping down the bar before Katrina could lean forward and lick the remains with her tongue. He took her by the arm. "C'mon, let's go somewhere else and talk."

"Go talk to your hockey buddies," said Katrina. "I'm going to Mexico with Heidi."

Heidi straightened and stared at Katrina, figuring the girl would've already forgotten the idea in her drunkenness.

"Like hell you are," said Tate.

Katrina glared at him. "Watch me."

Tate glared right back. "Watch *me*."

He slammed a bill down on the bar, gave Katrina one last furious look, and strode out the door.

2   SNOW DAY – AGAIN

A month earlier, in deepest, darkest January, Katrina had stared out the window of her salon at a giant neon red palm that glowed through the driving snow like an inviting beacon. It was just about the only thing she could see through the blizzard.

She considered closing early. There'd been hardly any action all day, and the few pedestrians struggling through the snow weren't interested in hair cuts right now; their main concern was keeping their heads warm and dry until they could reach the warmth of home or a welcoming pub.

It reminded her of the day two years ago when a regular client of hers named Duncan had come in and set forth a storm of events that changed her life.

"Weird, isn't it?" said Kevin's voice behind her, and Katrina jumped. "That place is always open, even during a snowstorm, but I've never seen anyone go in."

It took a moment for Katrina to clear her thoughts and realize her feature stylist was referring to the psychic shop across the street. She turned to him with a scoff.

"I don't wonder. Those places are total B.S., if you ask me."

"Oh, I don't know about that," said Kevin slyly, keeping her waiting, as he liked to do until she was forced to ask about it. Kevin was a bit of a drama queen, but he was also extremely uplifting and entertaining. She'd often joked that he would have been a perfect employee for Life of the Party, the company she'd worked for a couple of summers ago, which provided beautiful or gregarious escorts for private parties. But Kevin would always put a hand on his hip, thrust his head up in disgust and retort, "Sweetie, they could never have afforded me."

"I'm waiting," said Katrina with a roll of the eyes. "Don't tell me you actually went in there?"

"Of course I did. How could a drama queen resist?" He ignored Katrina's snort. "Besides, I was feeling desperate and lonely and wondering if I'd ever meet the man of my dreams ever since Ron and I…" Kevin trailed off and Katrina was afraid he might start to cry. But he took a deep breath and continued, now excited at telling the story.

"Creepy décor, all black with red velvet curtains, ancient photos that looked like witches. And the psychic, Madame Mesmeralda, was a shrivelled little old lady from the old country, just like in some old Hollywood movie. She even had a wart on her chin with a hair growing out of it."

"Oh, be serious!" scoffed Katrina, though her curiosity drove her to stare through the snow at the glowing palm.

"Dead serious," proclaimed Kevin in a spooky voice.

"Ha-ha. So what did she tell you? You haven't mentioned any man of your dreams, unless you've been hiding him, and I know you too well – you could never hide something like that from me."

"You'd be surprised." Kevin leered, as if remembering a particularly luscious encounter. "But seriously, she told me that I'd meet a tall, dark, handsome stranger."

"Gee, that's original. And did you?"

Kevin nodded. "I did. The very next day."

"And?" Katrina was leaning toward him now in anticipation, though she still had half an eye on the giant red palm.

"Well I did meet a tall, dark, handsome stranger." A strategic pause. "Only it happened to be a woman."

Katrina smacked Kevin on the shoulder and he feigned intense pain.

"It's true, I swear!" An evil grin crossed his face, and Katrina didn't like the look of it at all. He paused for dramatic effect, then turned her to the window and said, "I think you should go over there."

"What!"

"Sure. Right now. You've been wanting to work on your shyness, you told me yourself. An adventure like this is a brave move, it'll do you wonders!"

Katrina was shy. Very shy. She'd come out of her shell a bit since moving to Toronto from her small hometown of Pipton, but she still had to bolster her courage to talk to strangers and was intimidated by most new people she encountered.

Katrina had been shy with her clientele at first, but once she got to know them, things were fine. Besides, as her best friend Cathy had once told her, most of them were mainly interested in talking about themselves. Katrina just had to throw in the odd question and 'uh-huh' and 'oh, sure' and they'd be perfectly content.

And whenever Katrina found herself facing a shyness attack and at a loss for words with a new client, Kevin and her other stylist Marlene would chip in and keep the conversation flowing.

"You're nuts," Katrina said to Kevin.

"Fruit and nuts, but that's another story." Kevin ran to the back and grabbed Katrina's coat. He started shoving her arms into the sleeves despite her squirms and protests, and stuck a ten dollar bill in the pocket. "That should cover it."

"She must be really good at those prices."

"C'mon," urged Kevin. "Just try it."

Katrina got crafty. "Maybe if you close for me tonight."

Kevin groaned, knowing how boring that would be.

"What's in this for you, anyway?" asked Katrina.

"I'm just curious – and maybe you'll have more luck than I did."

"I'm not looking for a man," sniffed Katrina. "I already have one."

Kevin rolled his eyes as he pushed her out the door. "If you say so," he snorted.

3   THE MEN IN HER LIFE

Katrina knew that Kevin didn't approve of her boyfriend Tate, thought he was too blasé about the relationship and took Katrina for granted; thought he was too lackadaisical and not rich enough for a beauty like Katrina. Her friend Heidi felt the same way and often said so. Katrina's best friend, Cathy, kept mum; she knew better than to get in the middle, and besides, whatever made Katrina happy… But after the intense machismo of Jake, her man before Tate, Tate was really kind of refreshing.

Cathy had begun calling Katrina Rebound Girl some time ago, and Katrina couldn't help feeling that was somewhat true.

Cathy had said, "I think ever since I've known you, you've gone out with every kind of man imaginable. What's next? A psychopath? A superhero?"

Katrina had to admit she had bounced around a lot. First there'd been Len the biker, who she'd lived with before he took off to South America on an extended road trip. Then Jonathan, who she'd thought was her Prince Charming, until his actions put an end to that fantasy. Next had been Jake the cop, who'd seemed courtly and protective at first, until she realized the protection went too far - he was never able to turn off his cop radar long enough to make her feel that she wasn't about to be Miranda-ized.

He refused to share his work with her, even though she'd helped him with a couple of cases, one including work at a shady funeral parlour where they first met. What had once been help had turned to 'meddling', according to him.

In a way, she'd met Tate through Jake, when they all went to Leamington together with Cathy and her boyfriend Stewart and Tate's (at that time) girlfriend Iris. They solved a mystery, Iris and Tate broke up, Jake said he needed a break, and the break eventually led to a break-up.

Katrina met Tate again when it turned out he was living in her neighbourhood, walked by her salon and noticed a special on men's cuts. At the time Katrina had been trying to draw in more male clientele to expand business. Tate decided to go in for his twice-yearly cut (his long, wavy locks were precious to him), and he and Katrina started slowly dating, both of them wary after their break-ups.

They hit it off. He was so refreshing after the demands of Jake, so easy-going, the perfect antidote. He worked as a landscaper during Toronto's good weather (what there was of it), and the rest of the time did the odd cabinetry job for friends.

The only problem was that Katrina had started to feel that Tate was so laid-back and unpossessive that she didn't feel wanted at all. Though on the other hand, she sometimes wondered if she'd been treating him the same way, unconsciously holding him at arm's length because of her lousy track record with men. And she had to wonder sometimes, barely even admitting it to herself, if Kevin and Heidi were right about Tate; maybe she was just putting in time with him till someone better came along.

In the few months Katrina had been seeing Tate, she'd been busy.

Business at her salon, Kat's Kuts, had been booming ever since Katrina's sister, Kandy, a high-fashion model, did a couple of free TV and print ads to promote the place. People would come in hoping to see her there. What they didn't know was that Kandy showed up in T.O. about as often as Elvis. On the other hand, Katrina looked incredibly similar to Kandy, and people often mistook them in the salon, wondering why a high-paid model would be cutting hair.

Though Kandy had for a few years now been well-known among fashion fans, she'd become much more recognizable lately to the general public after appearing in a couple of horror flicks. They were only B movies, small roles, not much acting involved, but her looks had been noticed and she had high hopes.

"After all," Kandy had told Katrina over the phone almost a year ago, "Jessica Lange started off screaming in King Kong, and look how her career's turned out."

"Well," said Katrina awkwardly, having seen Kandy's films, "You can always go back to modelling."

21

"You'll see," retorted Kandy, "I'll get a break soon, a real acting role, not just screaming at the top of my lungs and running to escape the murderer. And why do they always make me fall down, anyway? It's always the damn chicks who fall down, isn't it?"

So now Katrina was getting stared at even more than usual. She'd always been stared at for her beauty, but this was something different. She gradually began to discover why.

One day, in a corner store, she'd been patiently waiting to pay for her milk and O.J. when a man next to her turned to her and said, "Kandy?" Katrina, confused, pointed to the rows and rows of chocolate bars on the shelves below the counter right in front of him. The man seemed not to notice. Katrina wondered if he was quite right in the head. He just kept staring at her.

"I just loved you in *Amazon Women of Borneo*. All that screaming! You've got quite a set of lungs on you." And he stared right at her breasts.

"Oh," said Katrina, caught off guard. "No, I'm – " She stopped herself before telling this whacko that she was Kandy's sister. That would only lead to more questions, and possibly a stalking.

"No," she said firmly, and she dropped her milk and O.J. on the counter and fled.

She'd managed to ram a couple of more chairs into the salon, and raised the prices a notch, but her customers didn't complain. Very few walk-ins anyway, the place was so busy. It was becoming more exclusive than Katrina liked, though her clientele definitely weren't snobs. She knew and liked all of them. And if she didn't like someone – well, it was her salon – she could just (politely) walk them out the door and out of her life. Or better yet, get Kevin or Marlene to do it.

The salon had been doing so well that Katrina had been thinking about expanding it. But not here on Broadview. She was crammed between a two-storey apartment building and a Greek restaurant that had been there forever. She'd have to look elsewhere.

"Why rent another place?" asked Tate one lazy Sunday afternoon when she'd been pondering the problem with him. "Just move out of your apartment upstairs and use that extra space."

"Oh, right," said Katrina. "Then find another apartment. You know what rents are like around here? Plus, I like living above the salon. No transit headaches, and I'm right there in case of emergency."

"So move in with me," said Tate, with all the romance of a guy telling his beer buddy he could crash on the couch for a couple of nights.

Katrina's jaw dropped. Tate saw her look of sheer amazement and his face crumpled just a little. He turned away and started clicking the remote, a sure sign of distress. Tate was the only heterosexual man Katrina had ever met who didn't click automatically, as if adjusting his crotch. Staring at the TV, he said, "No big commitment or anything, it's not like we're getting married or something." He darted a glance at her but her face was still numb. "I just think it makes sense, saves us both some money."

"Well, umm," Katrina muttered, forcing a smile on her face, her mind racing for an excuse, "that sounds like a great idea, but I don't think I could expand the salon to the second floor. Zoned for residential only, I think."

After moving in with her boyfriend Jonathan a couple of years ago, she'd vowed never again, not until she was sure. And she sure as hell wasn't sure with Tate. Did she feel strongly enough about him to make that kind of commitment? She'd always had a great time with him, he was very funny and laid-back, such a relief after Jake. And he certainly wasn't laid-back in bed.

Neither one of them had said those three scary "I love you" words, and Katrina wasn't sure she'd even want to hear them. After leaving the demands and over-possessiveness of Jake, she'd just (finally) regained her independence. Was she really willing to risk losing it all over again?

"Oh," said Tate, turning away and pretending to focus on the TV. "Too bad. It could've been fun."

Fun, thought Katrina. All her relationships had started out that way, and they'd all turned into dismal realities. Her track record with men sucked. And would Tate ever be more than a fond time-waster?

Well, this was all 20/20 hindsight. It would be a helluva lot easier if she could see into the future. What the hell, she thought, as she trudged through the slush across the street, her large feet helping her manoeuver through the snowbanks. She stared at the giant neon red palm in front of her and thought, maybe someone else could see into the future for her.

Maureen P. Moore

4   PSYCHIC OR PSYCHO?

Katrina stood in the tiny vestibule of the psychic shop and brushed the snow off her hair and coat and stomped her boots. Now that she was actually inside, her nerve had vanished. She considered scurrying right out again, but she knew Kevin would be watching from across the street. Maybe she could step in, throw the woman her ten dollars, and sneak out the back door. But no, Kevin would be expecting a full report in the morning, and there was no way around it. Besides, even though she'd never admit it to anyone else, she had hopes that there really was something to all this. She took several deep breaths, pushed open the door to a tinkling little bell, and carefully stepped inside.

Kevin couldn't have been more wrong about the psychic. Oh sure, the décor was what he'd described, black and red velvet and spooky old photographs, but the person who sat at a table with a red tablecloth was nothing like he'd mentioned.

She couldn't have been more than nineteen, and she was in the midst of painting her fingernails a very deep purple.

"Hi there!" she chirped, after blowing on a fingernail. "I'm Minnow."

Minnow? thought Katrina as she glanced around the room. Wasn't that the name of a small fish? She looked back at the girl. "I'm….I'm Katrina, I'm here to see the psychic."

"Oh!" said Minnow, as if surprised to get the business. "That's me!"

"I was expecting someone – "

"Older?" Minnow put the brush back in the nail polish bottle and set it aside. "My grandma used to be the psychic, but she passed on about a year ago, and my mom took over. But she likes her winters in Florida, so I do it part-time, to keep the business going while she's away."

"Oh," said Katrina, looking beyond Minnow in the hopes of finding the back door.

Minnow seemed to think Katrina was inspecting the place, because she said, "I know it's kind of gloomy in here, but my mom is like that, too. The old country, you know. I tried to cheer the place up, add a bit more colour, brighten it up, but she wouldn't hear of it."

She frowned as she fingered a black silk tassel on one of the drapes. "I suppose it's what people expect."

Minnow sensed Katrina's skittishness and urged her to sit down. Katrina, after hearing the spiel, knew she'd feel guilty if she didn't go ahead with things now.

Minnow sighed. "Not that I'm an interior decorator or anything. I'm actually studying fashion design."

That figured, thought Katrina. The girl wore black from head to toe, including a black beret, which Katrina figured was supposed to add to the psychic allure. Instead, with her deathly white face, darkly lined eyes and bright red lips, she looked more like a mime.

Seeing Katrina's doubtful look, Minnow piped up, "But I have the gift, no question about that."

Katrina stared at the empty table between them. "Isn't there supposed to be a crystal ball or tarot cards or something?" she asked.

Minnow giggled. "Oh no – not unless the client absolutely insists. I always thought all that stuff was a bunch of hocus-pocus anyway. I just take your hands and feel your energy."

"What if there isn't any?" joked Katrina.

Minnow stared at her as if she didn't understand. Not much of a one for humour, Katrina guessed. Or else just plain dim-witted. Was a stupid psychic as good as a smart one? Did it matter?

"Give me your hands," ordered Minnow, as she held out her own.

Katrina raised her hands from her lap and placed them on the table. They were trembling a little from nerves, and her fingers landed on top of Minnow's.

"Careful!" snapped Minnow, and Katrina wondered if she'd somehow screwed up the psychic forces.

"My fingernails," admonished Minnow. She gave them a once-over, determined the purple polish was safe, and took Katrina's hands in hers.

Katrina jumped in her seat. A live current seemed to crackle from the psychic's fingertips. Was this some kind of trick? Had the girl been rubbing her shoes against the carpet to give her a shock? But no, it was more long-lived than that. Suddenly Katrina felt afraid, as if she'd been thrown into some other realm, a dark and menacing one. Ancient spells and witchcraft seemed to hover in the air. "Your birthday," Minnow mumbled, her eyes closed. Katrina leaned closer to hear her. "Your 24th birthday…it's coming soon, right?"

"In a month," said Katrina, shocked. How could this girl know how old she was? "What about it?" she asked, grabbing Minnow's hands harder. Minnow seemed to have forgotten about her manicure. She increased her grip too, and her closed eyes appeared to be rolling around in their sockets.

"The time approaching your 24th birthday…It will be…it will be a time…"

"A time? Yes?"

"A time…"

"A time, yes," repeated Katrina anxiously, leaning forward in her seat.

"A time…of great upheaval."

"Upheaval? What kind of upheaval?"

Minnow took in a deep breath, as if preparing for the second coming. "You will meet a dark, handsome stranger."

Katrina jerked back and pulled her hands away. "Oh, come on!" she said. "You're not serious!"

Minnow's blue eyes sprung open, and her hands relaxed. "What? Did I say something wrong?"

"Dark, handsome stranger?" snorted Katrina. "Surely you can do better than that for my ten bucks."

"Ten?" said Minnow, miffed. "I don't know who told you that, but it's gone up to fifteen. We have operating costs, you know."

Katrina glanced around the shabby room and wondered what those costs could be. "Okay," she agreed. "For fifteen bucks you can at least say a *tall*, dark, handsome stranger."

Minnow looked dismayed. "Did I forget the tall part? Sorry."

"Well, I just don't want to end up with a Nigerian dwarf."

"Okay," nodded Minnow. "Then he's tall. You're tall, so I guess you want him tall, too. But I could make him short if you want. Some women like that, it makes them feel more powerful. That's what I read in *Cosmo*, anyway."

"How can you *make* him anything?" asked Katrina.

"It's not for me to say," said Minnow, staring humbly down at her hands, though Katrina suspected she was inspecting her nail polish. "It's the gift."

"The gift, sure, okay. Is there anything else I should know?"

Minnow closed her eyes again and took Katrina's hands. After a moment she said, "On your 24th birthday, you will discover who you truly love."

"Who I truly love! But I don't love any – " Katrina stopped with a jolt. *Did* she love Tate and not even know it? Had she freaked out at the idea of moving in with him because deep down she felt more for him than she'd like to admit? Or was she supposed to fall in love with this tall dark stranger guy? She asked Minnow, who'd returned to the real world, but she just shook her head.

"I can only tell you what the gift tells me. The rest you'll have to figure out for yourself."

"That's a big help," sniffed Katrina, rising from her chair. "Now you've got me all freaked out."

Minnow shrugged. "That's the risk you take when you step through the door and meddle with the psychic forces." She stood up, motioning Katrina to do the same. "God, I need a smoke. That'll be fifteen bucks – cash."

5   A MONTH IN HELL

The next month was hell. Katrina hadn't told Tate about her session with the psychic because of the 'you'll discover who you truly love' part. She wasn't sure if she loved him, and she sure as hell wasn't sure if he loved her. Yes, he'd asked her to move in with him, but the glib way he'd done it…Though she did remember the hurt look on his face when she'd said no.

And she could just imagine his reaction if she skipped that part and told him of The Great Upheaval.

Tate: "You believe some crackhead?"

Katrina: (correcting) "CrackPOT. And she's not. She's a psychic, she knows what she's talking about. I could feel her power."

Tate: "You could feel your wallet being emptied for no reason. It's all a bunch of psychic-babble if you ask me."

Then he'd turn back to the hockey game on TV.

Pre-psychic, their relationship had been light and breezy. Post-psychic was a nightmare. The words repeated themselves over and over in her head: "You will discover who you truly love."

She didn't love Tate, did she? And if it wasn't Tate who she truly loved, did that mean she was going to fall head-over-heels for some random guy in the next month? The 'dark handsome stranger' the psychic had mentioned? It hardly seemed likely.

Katrina's emotions ping-ponged all over the place.

One day she'd want to cling on to Tate with all her might, in case he was the one she 'truly loved', and she might risk losing him with her cavalier attitude – she hadn't exactly jumped for joy when he asked her to move in with him. She knew that if the tables were turned, that would probably be a deal-breaker for her.

But the next day she'd want to run for the hills, certain she didn't have deep feelings for Tate, and she should be holding out for that tall dark stranger dude the psychic mentioned – even if it did sound like a lot of B.S.

So poor Tate was at the receiving end of all this – one day smothered, the next ignored – without a clue why Katrina was acting so crazy. She talked incessantly about her upcoming birthday, made constant hints. Cathy had even told Katrina that he'd asked her for the reason behind Katrina's erratic behavior – but Cathy had wisely given him a tight-lipped "You'll have to ask her yourself."

Katrina was in such a kerfuffle over the whole thing that she became even klutzier than usual the more she fretted. One day, after bumping into the same salon chair three times in an hour and dropping a blow dryer on the floor, Kevin said, "Maybe we should change the name of this place from Kat's Kuts to Kat's Klutz."

Katrina had told Kevin, of course, about the psychic, and he'd been delighted. "Discover who you truly love! How thrilling! I'm all for it, sweetie!" And he'd started staring at the door to the salon every time it opened, hoping to see a tall, dark, handsome stranger. Katrina told him he was being ridiculous, but she found herself jumping every time the door opened too. When she'd finally admonished Kevin, saying, "This is ridiculous, we have to stop this nonsense," he'd replied, "I only want to see you with the right man, Kitty-Kat." When Katrina burst into tears, he finally shut up and stopped staring at the door for all of an hour. After Katrina threatened him with a month of closing shifts, that is.

Katrina had also told Heidi, who said, "I told you there was someone better out there for you."

"So you actually believe this psychic B.S.?" said Katrina doubtfully.

"Sure – why not? Anything that will open your eyes and get you away from The Slug."

"Stop calling him that," said Katrina. "He works."

"Yeah – half the year, if that."

Katrina wanted to tell Heidi that wasn't true, Tate wasn't exactly the Energy Bunny, but it wasn't as if he sat on the couch all day drinking beer and watching the Sports Network (well, not all the time).

"He calls me The Princess," snorted Heidi.

"He's just jealous of your money," said Katrina. Heidi's sweet grandmother had left her a fair inheritance, as well as a place just down the street from Katrina's on Broadview, a two-storey building with an apartment on top and a business below. Heidi had turned the business into a travel agency.

Katrina had never understood Heidi's antipathy toward Tate. Everybody liked Tate. Well, everyone except Kevin, who she sensed was jealous of him, since she spent more time with Tate now than him (aside from work, of course).

Or maybe Heidi was jealous because she didn't have a boyfriend. Not that it seemed to bother her. Heidi always had at least one guy going at a time – sometimes two or three - Katrina didn't know how she kept track of them all. And Bad Boys, all of them. Maybe that was it. Tate wasn't a Bad Boy (though Katrina got the idea that maybe he used to be), and Heidi simply didn't find him interesting. Katrina put the thought aside. Ruminating on Heidi's love life could keep you occupied on a desert island for years.

Cathy, when told the story, asked questions like the actress she was, wondering about Minnow's personality, the ambience, Katrina's gut feelings. But after a couple of weeks of the subject (Katrina wouldn't stop talking about it), they'd grown bored with it and interrupted Katrina whenever possible. She'd become fretful and self-obsessed around her friends. She was beginning to feel like a social pariah.

So finally, a week before her 24th birthday, Tate had had enough. Tate, usually so understanding and undemanding, told her he didn't want to see her until she got her shit together – or at least was willing to talk to him about it. Don't call me, I'll call you.

What was a girl to do?

Maureen P. Moore

6   WAITING FOR A PLANE

On the Friday morning after Katrina's argument with Tate at the Grub, Katrina and Heidi sat in the departure lounge of the airport, waiting for the announcement for the flight to Huatulco. Katrina vaguely remembered sleeping on Heidi's couch and being awakened by her to catch the airport limo. She'd even managed to stand upright long enough to take a shower. But beyond that…things were pretty much a blur. Katrina turned to Heidi for help remembering. Heidi could hold her liquor much better than Katrina could, and listening to her was like watching a movie about a stranger unfold from the night before. Slowly, Katrina started to remember bits and pieces.

After the last margarita, they'd wisely switched to beer (which, at least in Katrina's case, was far less gulp-able). Katrina insisted on going to Mexico with Heidi, and Heidi had tried to dissuade her.

"What about Tate?"

"The hell with him."

"Okay…but what about the salon?"

"Kevin will take care of it," Katrina had said, "I'll make sure of that."

"And how will you do that?" Heidi asked.

"I'll call him right now," Katrina had mumbled. She pawed her phone out of her purse, but the batteries, as usual, were dead. No techno-geek was she. She could never remember to recharge the damn thing. Heidi had handed Katrina her phone.

Katrina, slumped beside Heidi on one of the plastic waiting room chairs, sat up – well, sort of. She almost slumped down again immediately, her head pounding.

"I think I remember that part!" she cried.

"Bravo!" said Heidi, clapping.

"No, seriously," said Katrina, grabbing her friend's arm. "I called Kevin, and he was at a club or something."

"Something," muttered Heidi.

"There was loud music in the background," remembered Katrina, "house music. He sounded half in the bag. I told him about going to Mexico, but – "

She halted there, unsure. Heidi filled her in.

"But you were afraid he wouldn't remember, so you decided to slip a note under the door of the salon, which he'd be sure to see as soon as he opened up."

"That's right!" said Katrina. Then she slumped some more. "He seemed really happy that I'd had a fight with Tate."

"Surprise, surprise," said Heidi.

"Yeah – the two of you should get together and have a party to celebrate," said Katrina. "Then I told him to get Marlene to cover for me too, he knows what she's like, don't let her get away with any excuses."

"Then," said Heidi, "we went up to your place, to pack really quick, before the wolf showed up at the door."

"The wolf?" asked Katrina, queasy, wondering if she should make another run for the bathroom.

"Tate. You didn't want him to suddenly show up while you were still there. I helped you pack, and you kept complaining you didn't know where your summer clothes were, and I told you all you really needed were your bikini, passport and bank card, we could always buy stuff when we got there."

Heidi sighed. "And of course you couldn't remember where your passport was. You kind of pointed at a drawer, and I went looking for it, and when I found it and got back to you, you were snoring on the bed."

"Sorry," muttered Katrina, reddening.

"Then," said Heidi, rolling her eyes, "you said you wanted to spend the night in your own bed, it was so cosy, and I reminded you that Tate could show up at any minute, and he'd convince you not to go." She sighed again. "Not that I would've dissuaded him. So anyway, I dragged you off the bed, shoved everything in your purse and duffel bag, and hauled you over to my place."

"You're a goddess," said Katrina. "Thank you."

"More like an indulgent idiot," said Heidi. "Somehow I managed to drag you into my office with me and I was able to book you a last-minute flight." She snorted in dismay. "Which ended up costing less than mine."

"Sorry," said Katrina. She roused herself a little. "Where are we going, anyway?"

"For the tenth time," said Heidi, "it's a little town called Pacifico, north of Puerto Escondido. A couple of my clients raved about it, said it had that 'not yet discovered' feel to it, so I thought I'd check it out." She smiled coyly. "Purely for business reasons, of course."

"Of course," said Katrina.

"Anyway," said Heidi, "there are some cute little cabanas across from the beach which one client highly recommended. There's a beach strip with bars and restaurants, and if that gets boring, the main town is only a few minutes away, with lots of shops and authentic Mexican restaurants. Not much to it, but it has a great beach, great beach bars, and tons of lovely surfer boys."

"Surfer boys," Katrina repeated dreamily, then she started to gag, jumped off her chair and sprinted for the washroom.

When Katrina returned, Heidi commented on her breath and offered a stick of gum. Katrina looked at it sourly and said, "I don't think I can handle that right now." She glanced at her watch. "When the hell are they going to start boarding? We're supposed to take off in twenty minutes." She sighed, closing her eyes. "I'll be so glad to get out of this frigging city."

Finally, the announcement was made for initial boarding: children, the elderly, the handicapped. Katrina roused herself and grabbed Heidi's arm.

"I'm feeling pretty handicapped right now," she said. "Let's go."

Maureen P. Moore

7   LIFTOFF

After settling into their seats, Katrina insisting on a window seat since she'd only flown once before, to Cuba, they both fell into a deep sleep. After a while, they were awakened by a flight attendant offering stale subs – mystery meat or vegetarian.

Katrina turned up her nose, but Heidi said, "You'd better eat something. It's a long trip, and who knows when we'll get around to eating again."

Heidi asked for the vegetarian, and Katrina reluctantly did likewise. Still hurting, she ordered a Bloody Caesar. Heidi asked for a bottle of water.

"You're not going to join me?" asked Katrina.

"I get dehydrated on planes. I'll have a drink a little later," said Heidi. She unwrapped her sandwich and wrinkled her nose. "Might want to get rid of the onions," she said.

"Why?" asked Katrina. "They look like the tastiest part of this hideous thing."

"You never know who you might meet," said Heidi, dropping the onions into the air sickness bag.

"Sure I do," said Katrina sarcastically, "A tall, dark, handsome stranger."

She took a long sip of her Caesar and opened her mouth to speak, and Heidi thought, oh no, here we go again, The Great Upheaval. Katrina's babbling for the last month about the whole psychic shit had been driving Heidi crazy. Maybe on Sunday when her birthday rolled around and the sky hadn't fallen, Katrina would realize how silly she'd been and get back to normal. She used to be a lot of fun.

"Oh, look," Heidi said quickly, pulling out headphones from her bag under the seat. "There's a movie on!"

"It's half over!" said Katrina, taking another sip of her drink. "How can you watch a movie at a time like this?"

Heidi ignored her, slipped on her headphones, and started chewing distastefully on her sandwich. She'd heard of the days when tasty, hot meals were available on all flights, wine included. Sometimes they even had real china. Oh well, that was the price you paid for not paying much, she supposed.

Katrina finished pouring the tiny vodka bottle into her clamato juice and glanced sidelong at Heidi, who seemed absorbed by the movie. In fact, everyone did. They were even laughing. Katrina didn't have the attention span to watch a movie; she wanted to talk. Maybe if she babbled enough at Heidi, she'd finally take off her headphones and listen.

Katrina wasn't sure why Heidi wasn't drinking. Maybe it was a way of avoiding talking. Heidi had two very long hollow legs, she was tall, she had gorgeous wavy dark red hair and tawny skin with just a smattering of adorable freckles; and to add insult to injury she had magnificent boobs. Katrina was no slouch in that department but compared to Heidi she felt downright flat-chested.

Katrina had met Heidi when she'd hesitantly come in for a cut and style one day, explaining that her regular stylist had closed up shop to move to the Bahamas with a gorgeous sailor, and she was looking for someone new. She didn't seem to be expecting much, but Katrina's cut had pleased her, and they'd hit it off. Before they knew it, they were meeting at the Grub a couple of times a week after work. Heidi wasn't the cosy/cuddly/huggy type of friend that Cathy was, but she was very entertaining, and Katrina admired her sophistication and all her travel stories. She could be a bit bitchy sometimes, especially when she was drunk, but that was just part of her M.O., and Katrina had learned to mainly ignore it.

Katrina went over in her mind the argument with Tate from the night before, wondering how it had all gone so terribly wrong, and what she was doing flying to Mexico with Heidi instead of talking to Tate in an adult way. Well, he was the one who'd taken off in a huff, not her. She would've been willing to conduct a reasonable conversation – wouldn't she? At the moment, she'd rather not think about it. She ordered another Caesar instead. After all, they were a lot smaller than the Margaritas last night, and she was beginning to feel a whole lot better.

Katrina paid for the drink and tried clumsily to open the mini-bag of pretzels the flight attendant had given her. Who the hell invented these packages, anyway? You practically needed a chain saw to open the damn things. She glanced around for the flight attendant, but she was long gone, and Katrina, starving now since she'd only nibbled at the crummy sandwich, felt desperate. Angrily she used all her strength and ripped at the bag, her elbow smacking Heidi in the ear and yanking off her headphones.

"Jesus!" cried Heidi, looking over at Katrina. "What the hell is wrong with you?" The bag had opened, all right – the pretzels had spilled all over Heidi's lap.

Katrina tried to avoid Heidi's glare by glancing guiltily up at the TV screen and saw that the credits were rolling on the movie. Now she didn't feel so bad. At least she hadn't interfered with that.

"Sorry," muttered Katrina, grabbing pretzels from Heidi's lap, until Heidi smacked her hand and brushed the whole mess onto the floor. "Don't suppose I could get any more of those, do you?"

"On this shit airline? They'd probably charge you five bucks."

"Not if we order another drink."

Heidi glanced at Katrina's two empty vodka bottles, and her half empty glass. "Maybe you should wait on that."

"I was talking about you."

Heidi stretched, then put the earphones back in her bag beneath the seat.

"Why not? I think I have one of those progressive hangovers. I felt fine when I got up, but now I'm starting to feel like shit."

"So," said Katrina when Heidi had settled into a vodka and O.J. ,"do you think I'm crazy to fly off to Mexico? Should I just break up with him? What?"

"Just wait and see," said Heidi.

"Wait and see? You sound like my mother."

"Take the week away and enjoy the sun and try not to think about it. I'm sure Tate isn't going anywhere."

"I'm not so sure."

Heidi turned to stare at Katrina. "What's that supposed to mean?"

Katrina sighed and sipped on her Caesar. "The thing is, Tate and I have this agreement."

"Agreement?"

"Well, I got the idea he was a bit of a player back in his early twenties, and I wasn't exactly a virgin myself. So when we started going out, I told him I had one rule: no talking about past relationships. I've done it before, and it's always a disaster."

"Oh, that agreement. You've mentioned that before, and I'm with you on that one. You mention one little ex, and they want to know all the details. They also start thinking you've been with everyone in town and half of Canada.

"Yeah," said Katrina, shaking her head ruefully. "So I made this pact with Tate, and he wasn't thrilled with it, but he went along."

"Really?" said Heidi, sitting up in her seat. "I didn't know this part of it before. So you don't know about any of his past lovers?"

Katrina shook her head. "But now I'm beginning to wonder if he might've gone back to his old ways."

"Oh?" Heidi leaned over so abruptly she spilled a bit of her drink and quickly mopped it up with her cocktail napkin.

"He didn't call me for a whole week – that's just not like Tate."

"Well you have to admit you weren't exactly – "

"I know, I know," said Katrina with a sigh. "I was being weird and freaked out. So I started thinking…"

Heidi leaned forward expectantly.

"I started thinking maybe he was seeing someone from his past."

Heidi looked off into the distance, smiling a little.

"You think that's funny?"

"No, not at all." Heidi turned to Katrina. "Sorry, it just made me think of someone I used to know. You were saying?"

"Well, he could be screwing around on me with somebody from his past, for all I know, since I don't know anything about his past."

"Hmm," said Heidi thoughtfully. "Why do you think it's someone from his past?"

Katrina shrugged. "Just a feeling. And I don't dare ask him, 'cause if he is, I don't want to know, and if he isn't, I'm afraid I might be putting ideas in his head." Katrina leaned back and gave a feeble laugh. "It's probably nothing, I'm probably just freaking out again. Anyway," she sighed, "I'm tired of talking about it." She laughed at an audible exclamation of relief from Heidi. "What's going on with you in the men department? You've been acting kind of strange lately yourself."

Heidi looked taken aback. "What do you mean by that?"

Katrina finished her drink and looked around for the flight attendant. She was beginning to get the idea the woman was hiding from her. Maybe she'd try the other one, the gay guy. He'd actually smiled at her when he caught her babbling away to herself.

Katrina turned to Heidi. "I haven't seen you making out with a single guy at the Grub in the last few weeks. What's with that?"

Heidi snorted. "As if you would've noticed, with your Great Upheaval going on."

"But I did. I know I've had my head up my own butt, but that was kind of hard not to see. Every time Tate and I were in there you were sitting all prim and prissy by yourself, not even swivelling your head." Katrina chuckled. "Of course, you could've been with ten guys last night and I wouldn't't've noticed."

Heidi turned away from Katrina and looked across the aisle for a long moment, thinking. She noticed the gay flight attendant and motioned for another round of drinks, and was rewarded with a wink, then leaned into Katrina in a confiding manner.

"The thing is, I decided it was time to break my Bad Boy pattern. So I started seeing a therapist."

"You?" said Katrina, sitting up and nearly knocking heads with Heidi. "You live for Bad Boys, you thrive on Bad Boys, you – "

"Yeah, yeah, I get the picture," cut in Heidi. "But you know, it's like everything else: too much of something and it's just not fun anymore. And they've stopped being fun for me. But I still keep doing it. I figured, there's got to be a reason. So I started seeing – " She coughed delicately, as if choking a bit on the word, "Bronwyn."

"Bronwyn? That sounds like a soap opera name."

"Does it?" Heidi hesitated a moment, then added, "Well it fits her. She's very classy, very reserved. Waspy, I guess. The thing is, she told me I had to break my pattern, stop beating myself up, get on with my life."

"Is it working?"

Heidi gave a glum smile. "I'm not sure. I haven't seen any Bad Boys lately. But I have dated a couple of the most boring men in the universe."

Katrina frowned. "God, Heidi, I'm sorry. What kind of friend am I? I didn't even know you were going through this, I've been so self-obsessed with everything."

Heidi patted Katrina's hand. "It's okay. I understand."

Katrina perked up a little. "Well, there's gotta be something in between the bad and the boring. I thought Tate was, but now..." She trailed off and turned to Heidi. "Oh God, I'm sorry. There I go again, blabbing away about myself." She glanced up at the arrival of the flight attendant and accepted the drinks he handed her. She passed one to Heidi. "Let me at least pay for these." She reached into her purse.

Heidi lifted her glass in a toast. "Well you know what? Why don't we forget all these stupid man troubles for a week? We'll lie in the sun, drink pina coladas, and when we get back, we can both figure out what to do about it all."

They clicked plastic glasses, turned toward the window, and stared down at the mountains of Mexico.

Maureen P. Moore

8   JOE'S CABANAS

They lucked out and hit the green light at customs and didn't get
their bags checked, which Katrina realized afterward was a damn
good thing, since her duffel actually belonged to Tate, and the
last time they'd used it was to go up to a friend's cottage.
Knowing Tate, it could still have some pot — or at least
remnants – in it. She'd have to remember to give it a good wash
before she packed to go home. Or throw it in the ocean. Or burn
it.

They both used the ATMs inside the airport to get some
pesos, then grabbed a few cold cans of beer and found a cab with
a flat rate for the two-hour ride to their destination.

Katrina took a sip of beer and studied the gold can.
"Hey, this is called Pacifico. Isn't that the name of the place
we're going to?"

"Yep," said Heidi, rolling down the window. "Man, I
love this heat."

"I love the beer. Damn tasty. I hope the town's as good
as the beer." Katrina took another swallow from her can and
said, "You think we can actually stay drunk for an entire week?
You know, I do have a tendency to puke".

Heidi turned away from the window and considered her.
"You managed not to hurl last night." She patted Katrina's
shoulder. "Well done. Yeah, I think we can stay drunk as long as

we want. Drinking, eating, shopping – if I'm ever sober enough. Drunken shopping's more fun anyway."

Katrina shrugged, having no experience in this area. On her one previous trip down to Cuba with Jake, he'd held onto the purse-strings and had bought her only a tiny shell bracelet. Cheap bastard. "I suppose," she said. "I guess you never know what you'll end up buying."

"Tell me about it," said Heidi. "I bought about twenty ceramic plates one time, then when it was time to pack and go home, I realized it would cost ten times what they were worth to ship them, and I sure as hell couldn't put them in my luggage."

"You could afford it," said Katrina.

Heidi shrugged. "I'm cheap that way. Anyway, when I looked at them sober, they were totally hideous."

Katrina leaned back in her seat and peered out at the palm trees and Corona signs, the mountains glowing with the lowering sun. "Wish we could've gotten here earlier, so I could see things better." She sighed contentedly. "But no worries — I'll see it all tomorrow. And this is the life. Heat, sun, sand. No snow, no work, no…Tate…." Her voice caught a little, and Heidi glanced over at her and patted her hand.

"Maybe we shouldn't talk about Tate."

"I suppose you're right. No talking about Tate, no thinking about Tate, no – "

"No thinking at all," added Heidi.

Katrina sipped some more beer. "Now you're talking."

It was about an hour after sunset when the cab pulled off the main road and onto a dirt one, blowing dust everywhere. Katrina coughed and rolled up her window.

"This is the resort?" she asked dubiously.

"It's not a resort; it's a beach town. I told you that," said Heidi as she rolled up her own window.

They passed a strip club and a cantina full of rough looking cowboys. "These aren't the only bars, are they?" asked Katrina. "I was kind of hoping to make it back to Toronto in one piece."

"Relax, we're right on the beach, in the middle of the gringo strip. All you'll have to worry about is some surfer dudes and a bunch of backpackers."

"Oh, right – the surfer dudes," said Katrina. "You mentioned those earlier."

"So, you weren't totally comatose when I was talking to you," said Heidi. "Oh – that reminds me." She burrowed into her huge Chanel bag. Her hand emerged with a long strip of condoms. Katrina stared at them blankly.

"Now why on earth would I need those? Tate and I haven't used them in months." Katrina frowned. "Though now that you mention it, maybe I should've."

"You might need them with somebody else. The surfer boys seemed to grab your attention."

"For looking, that's all."

"Just take them," said Heidi, shoving the plastic strip into Katrina's hand.

Katrina, too tired and drunk to protest, merely shrugged, said, "Whatever," to stop Heidi from bugging her anymore, and thrust the condoms into the pocket of her shorts. Pressure on her bladder gave her a good excuse to change the subject.

"Where's this ocean you keep talking about? I swear I'm going to have to pee in it soon if we don't get where we're going."

The most obvious thing about Joe's Cabanas, besides the sign, was the square, thatch-roofed bar at the front of the complex. It was on the main beach road, across from the ocean. Beside the bar was a small office, and beyond, through the foliage, a dozen or so small cabanas around a kidney-shaped pool.

"This is it?" said Katrina, surprised and a little disappointed. "Somehow I thought you'd be the high-rise type, Heidi. You know, a swank condo on the beach, air conditioning, elevators, wide screen TV..."

Heidi grinned. "Don't let my refined good looks deceive you."

"Oh, right," said Katrina, "I've seen some of the men you've been with."

Heidi smacked her on the arm. "We are on the beach. And do you see any high-rises here? They've got a law in a lot of these places — no buildings higher than the tallest palm tree."

"It's kind of...rustic," said Katrina, noting the general run-down aspect to the place.

"But they tell me it's clean. Besides, I like rustic when I'm here, it feels more...Mexican. If I wanted condos I'd go to Florida." Heidi lowered her voice. "And don't tell any of my clients I said this, but I hate all-inclusives, period. Though there aren't any in this town anyway, thank God."

They got out and Heidi paid and over-tipped the cab driver, who was all smiles as he placed their luggage on the sidewalk. Heidi considered demanding him to carry the luggage the few metres to the office, but figured Katrina, always so polite, would think her rude, so she just shrugged to herself as the cabbie drove off, honking his horn.

Katrina turned toward the beach. She could hear the waves thundering against the shore, though she could barely see them. "That's the Pacific? Why the hell do they call it that? Doesn't pacific mean peaceful or something?"

"Beats me," said Heidi. "But it sure ain't the Caribbean."

Katrina nodded. "I can see that. That place we went in Cuba had water like a bathtub – and just about as ferocious." She took a step closer toward the beach. "I'm dying to go in there. I've never swum in the Pacific before."

Heidi tugged on her arm. "Well you're not going in there now. You won't be able to see, for one thing, and those boomers would kill you in your condition."

"I'm not drunk," protested Katrina, as she burped and threw the last of the beer cans into a garbage container on the street. She straightened up as best she could and picked up her duffel bag as she followed Heidi and her gigantic rolling suitcase up the path to the office.

As they entered and glanced around, Heidi said, "I just hope they have a spare cabana for you."

"Couldn't you have e-mailed?"

"They don't have e-mail," replied Heidi. "I had my friend call for my reservation a while ago; she speaks fluent Spanish."

"If they don't have anything," said Katrina, suddenly very tired, "we could always be roommates."

Heidi smiled indulgently. "Nothing against you, my sweet, but I'm hoping to get laid on this trip."

Katrina gave her the sternest look she could manage considering her drunken condition. "What about Bronwyn and the Bad Boys?"

Heidi glanced up and down the dirt beachfront street, where the only occupants were a couple of scruffy dogs and two local workmen passing by in the back of a pickup truck, leering at them. "There's got to be a good guy around here somewhere."

Teresa, the young Mexican woman who arrived at the ring of the bell on the desk, was incredibly sweet, luckily spoke broken English, and was happy to inform them that yes, there were free cabanas, though none of them were next to Heidi's. Heidi seemed happy about that, and Katrina couldn't really blame her. If she did get lucky, she wasn't going to want a solo Katrina right next to her, morosely listening to her every move.

Teresa showed Katrina a cabana across the pool from Heidi's, since it was shadier and a little more spacious than the others available. Before Katrina could even look inside, Heidi said it was great, they'd take it, and Teresa smiled and said she was finishing up soon for the day, if she could just have a credit card, they could finish the formalities in the morning. Heidi nudged Katrina, she reluctantly handed over the card, and Teresa gave both the girls keys, said good night and left.

Katrina would've liked to inspect some of the other cabanas, but she was so very tired. She picked up her duffel while Heidi left her humongous suitcase on the pathway around the pool, and stepped onto the little porch, which contained a hammock, a chair and table, and a giant water jug hanging upside down from a rusty iron stand.

"Is that water really safe?" asked Katrina, calling after Heidi, who'd already entered the cabana.

"A lot safer than any of the shit you're going to get from the sink," was Heidi's reply.

Katrina entered the cabana. There was a tiny kitchen, a desk and chair, and a bed surrounded by mosquito netting. Katrina rolled onto it, entwining her fingers in the netting.

"No way! This is just like in a movie!"

"Good thing, too," said Heidi, inspecting the wood slats of the cabana; they had cracks big enough for an iguana to waltz through.

Katrina dragged herself off the somewhat lumpy but very inviting bed and went to check out the bathroom.

"What on earth is this?" she asked Heidi, who followed and peered over her shoulder, trying not to laugh.

"The real Mexico," replied Heidi, enjoying Katrina's disbelief. There was no shower curtain, and the shower was mere inches from the toilet and the sink. "You can take a piss, brush your teeth, and have a shower all at the same time. It's what they call multi-tasking in Mexico." Heidi smiled innocently. "And there's also the cucarachas, the geckos, and the scorpions."

Katrina looked terrified.

"But don't worry," added Heidi quickly, afraid she might have gone overboard, "I haven't run into a scorpion yet - just shake out your shoes before you put them on."

Heidi left the bathroom. "I'm going to go over to my place and change out of these grungy clothes. Don't bother unpacking till tomorrow — we should enjoy ourselves tonight, our first night in May-hee-co. I'll meet you at the bar in five."

Katrina stood shivering in the tiny bathroom, despite the heat, her eyes darting around for scorpions and cucarachas. She noticed the drain on the floor by the sink, and wondered if anything could crawl up it. Taking a deep breath, she wiped at some smudged makeup under her eyes and ran her fingers through her wind-blown hair. Only as she turned from the mirror did she notice that the small, low window in the dimly lit bathroom was completely open to the bar and pool area. Horrified, she quickly hung a towel over the window, making the bathroom even dimmer, and thought the hell with it, she didn't know where anything in her duffel bag was and was too drunk to care; she'd go to the bar dressed the way she was.

When Katrina arrived unsteadily at the bar, Heidi was already perched on a stool, looking gorgeous and refreshed in a tiny dress. The only other customers were a cuddly couple and a tired old dog sleeping nearby.

Heidi turned to the middle-aged, bearish man behind the bar. "Katrina, this is Joe. He's the owner of this fine establishment."

"Owner, bartender, bouncer, handyman," said Joe, putting out his hand to shake Katrina's. "Nice to meet you ladies."

"You can call us girls," said Katrina, "we won't mind."

"Sure," agreed Heidi. "No one's ever called us ladies before." She glanced around, indicating the nearly empty grounds. Two people sat semi-comatose by the pool, sipping on cans of beer. "Where is everybody? I heard this was a pretty lively place."

Joe shrugged. "Everybody's probably having a siesta or gone out for dinner. Don't worry, it'll get hopping again in a little while." He pointed toward the unobstructed view of the dark ocean. "Best sunset in all of Mexico right here."

"C'mon, Joe," laughed Heidi. "You can't fool me; I'm a travel agent. We say that about everywhere."

Joe pretended to be offended. "Well in this case it's true."

Katrina yawned. "I'm sorry we missed it."

"Rough travel day?" asked Joe.

"Rough everything," said Katrina, looking away dejectedly.

Joe glanced at Heidi and she leaned on the bar with an overly bright smile. "How about a couple of pina coladas, start our trip off right? And not girly ones, either."

"Sure thing," said Joe, reaching for the rum. "Katrina, Heidi tells me you girls are from Toronto. Guess the weather's pretty sweet there right about now."

Katrina snorted, a sure sign she was tipsy. "Sweet as sneet – as in a sleet and snow combo."

Joe grinned as he started the blender. "I can relate to that – I'm from Wisconsin. Don't miss it one bit. Been here twenty years now."

"Lucky you."

"Well it's not bad work if you can get it."

Joe turned off the blender and handed them their drinks. "Enjoy. You stay in my cabanas, the first one's on the house."

Katrina seemed to perk up at the offer of free drinks. "We should've ordered triples," she said, smiling. "But don't worry, you'll be getting plenty of business from us this week."

"Too bad I won't be here for it," said Joe. "I'm going up to Puerto Vallarta after I close up here tonight. Taking a week off, see some friends. Craig'll be taking over the bar for me while I'm gone."

"Is he cute?" asked Heidi.

"Not as cute as me," grinned Joe, "but he'll do. You girls down here on your own?"

"Hopefully not for long," said Heidi coyly. "One of my clients told me there were a lot more men than women in this town."

Joe shook his head sadly. "Ain't that the truth. I'm married myself, but all my single friends tell me – " Teresa stepped out of the office and called to him and he said, "Be right back."

Katrina swivelled in her stool to face Heidi. "Now why do you say stuff like that? Speak for yourself."

"Oh come on, it wouldn't hurt you to flirt with somebody. What you need is a little affirmation."

"Affirmation? What's that, a Bronwyn word?"

"As a matter of fact, yes."

"Did Bronwyn supply you with all those condoms, too?"

"Of course not; they were sitting in my bedside table drawer. I thought they might come in handy."

"I don't think this Bronwyn lady's helping your Bad Boy problem much, Heidi."

"It's a process. Anyway, I was talking about you, not me. A little flirtation right now would do you wonders, stop you thinking about you-know-who so much."

"Okay, Heidi – if I see anyone I want to flirt with, I'll let you know."

"I don't need a report, Katrina." Heidi laughed. "Though if you want to fill me in, I'll be all ears."

Katrina glanced around the bar - still only the lone couple lapping away at each other. The man came up for air and nuzzled his girlfriend's neck. He saw Katrina staring at him, and she blushed and started to look away, but not before the man winked at her and ran his tongue over his lips. Katrina turned away in disgust. Heidi hadn't noticed; she was petting the dog.

"That report you mentioned, Heidi?" Katrina leaned down and took a long sip of her Pina Colada through her straw. "Not sure it's gonna happen."

9   THE BAD BOY

Pete jumped off the back of the pickup, where he'd been squeezed between two kids, two dogs, chickens, and several crates of close-to-rotting vegetables, grabbed his backpack and shouted "Muchas gracias!" with an added "asshole!" under his breath. Yeah, sure, he was grateful for the free lift, but would it have killed the jerk to drive him just a little further? Now he was stuck at least a couple of miles from the beach, on a dusty road, thirsty and tired as hell.

If the weather back in T.O. weren't so bad this time of year, he might've considered going home. But mid-February was no time to leave Mexico, no matter how broke you were. Not that he'd planned on being broke. But he'd gotten drunk in Zipolite and stayed in that frigging hammock joint. No wonder it only cost a few pesos a night. It was basically a thatch-roofed barn on the beach, three-sided, open to the sea, with poles to attach your hammocks. Nowhere to put your shit. So easy to be robbed blind. Which he was. How could he have been so damn drunk as to throw his jeans with most of his money and his phone on a hook by his hammock? At least he'd had enough sense to tuck his passport, return air ticket and a bit of money under his pillow or he'd really be in the shits now.

His old man had been no help at all. When he'd called him collect for a loan, just one more little loan, honest, the asshole had hung up on him. So much for family and love and loyalty. The old man wasn't getting a Father's Day card from him this year, that was for sure.

Pete had arrived in Mazatlan in early November, working his way down the Pacific coast of Mexico, steps at a time, down to Huatulco. Literally working. Not much, but he was a housepainter back home, so he did the odd jobs for ex-pats he met in bars, painting or fixing things up or whatever would help his trip along. He intended to stay until at least the end of March, when the snow in Toronto was almost history.

When he got to Puerto Escondido after the robbery, he'd thought at first maybe he could get some free food and lodging off the female tourists, but that didn't work. They all wanted local colour, it seemed, something they could brag to their friends about back home. Like, guess how many Mexicans I hooked up with on my vacation! He'd thought Jamaica was the place for that shit, Rent-a-Rastas and all that. Man, was he wrong. He'd started to feel like that loser from *Midnight Cowboy*. Next, he'd be standing on a street corner waiting to give B.J.'s to old men.

He'd done something he'd never done before: he stole. He robbed a couple of drunken tourists, figuring it was only karma, after all. He considered himself a basically honest person, but a guy had to eat and drink. It wasn't like he was taking their credit cards or anything, just a little cash.

But he'd started getting wary looks from some of the people he'd been hanging with, and decided it was high time to get out of town. Start heading north again. It was too cheap down here. Which was great for getting by, but bad for squeezing money out of anybody else. Too many surfers and backpackers. Even the ex-pats didn't seem to have much money. Too many cheap Canadians and not enough rich Americans. He'd have to head up to Acapulco, then maybe Puerto Vallarta. Lots of high-rises and all-inclusives and fancy restaurants there, none of this boho living.

He was tired of struggling with the language, too. He thought he would've picked up more Spanish by now, but his language skills obviously sucked. He could speak it a bit, but once they talked back to him, he just stared back like a deaf-mute. Did they have to talk so damn fast? He swore English speaking people didn't talk a mile a minute like that. Why did the Mexicans talk so fast when they moved so slow?

Pete sighed and adjusted his backpack as he trudged down the road. It was dark and poorly lit and he was sure he'd soon be stepping on a dog or a cow or falling into some deep ditch.

The honking of a horn and the glare of headlights made him turn around. A dusty shit-box of a car was speeding toward him. He stepped quickly aside, well aware of how most of the Mexicans drove: the faster and more reckless, the more macho.

The car suddenly veered toward him, and he jumped. The car stopped just short of him, and he heard wild laughter from inside.

"Hey, gringo, you should see the look on your face!"

Pete, who'd tripped and landed on his ass in the dust in his effort to escape, slowly got up and scowled at the driver, who'd rolled down his window to grin at him. He was expecting a toothless derelict, but the man was unexpectedly handsome, with flashing white teeth and an endearing smile.

"Thanks a lot," said Pete, "I think I just ripped my last pair of jeans."

"Let me look, amigo."

Pete warily turned around, afraid this might be some kind of joke, like a whole flock of headlights might suddenly flood his ass. But the man merely said, "No hay problema, you are good to go."

"Then I will," grunted Pete, starting down the road again. The car followed him.

"Hey, buddy, I was only going to offer you a ride!"

Pete stopped and squinted into the headlights. "Then why the hell didn't you say so? I thought you were trying to run me down."

The man grinned and reached over to open the door. "Well – maybe a little."

Pete warily got in, his backpack on his lap, and the man leaned over to adjust a bunch of colourfully woven hammocks on the back seat, then motioned for Pete to throw his bag there.

"My profession," he said proudly, as he started the car. "That is how I speak such good English. The tourists, they teach me." He flashed that gleaming grin again. "Mostly the ladies." He lit up a joint, took several deep puffs, then offered it to Pete. "Me, I am Ramon."

"Pete. Look, thanks for the ride, I didn't mean to be rude or anything but – "

"But you're not having such a good time here in Mexico, is that right?"

Pete inhaled deeply on the joint and said, "What was your first clue?"

"Sorry?"

Pete shook his head. "Nothing. Look, are you going toward the beach?"

"Anywhere you like, amigo." Ramon shrugged and took the joint back. "Except maybe Puerto Escondido. There, they do not like me so much."

"Yeah," nodded Pete. "Me neither. I just came from there. I was in Zipolite before that."

"Nice town. Too many hippies for me, though. They have no money, those kids." Ramon turned to study Pete. "So, where you want to go? Not the Hilton, eh?" He laughed hard at his own joke and nearly swallowed the joint. He threw it out the window as he caught his breath.

"Anything cheap that's close to the beach. If there's nothing too cheap I'll just sleep on the beach."

71

"Not a good idea," said Ramon. "The policia, they patrol the beach here at night." Again, that grin. "For men like you. No freebies for the turistas."

"Okay, so we're back to something cheap." Now it was Pete's turn to grin. "Unless you know a bar where I might meet a nice turista who'd offer me her room for the night."

"Joe's – "

Pete stopped him. He'd pronounced it 'hoes'. "I'm not looking for a ho, a hooker, I just want…"

"No, Hoe's, Hoe's…" Ramon saw Pete's blank look and suddenly realized his mistake. "I mean Joe's, with a J, Joe's Cabanas. Joe's bar is the place to go this time of night. Everything else on the beach closes real early. Then you have to go into town, where there is no ocean breeze and it is very hot."

Ramon shrugged. "Not that it's far, only a few minutes by car, but – "

"Screw it," said Pete, "I'm tired, I don't want to go to some frigging disco or surfer bar. Let's go to this Joe's place. If I really have to, I'll even pay for a room."

"And a beer for me?" suggested Ramon with a wide white grin. "For the ride?"

Pete couldn't help but laugh. Ramon certainly had a sly charm. "Sure, buddy, a beer for you. You're a lot better company than a chicken bus."

10 THE NAUGHTY GIRL

Ramon parked his car on what Pete assumed, by the sound of the crashing waves, was the main beach road. It was dark. Very dark. The only light came from a dim streetlight that looked miles away, and all he could see out his window was a crumbling, abandoned old hotel, probably the victim of a hurricane.

Pete suddenly felt paranoid, not helped along by the pot he'd smoked with Ramon. He turned suspiciously to him. "Hey, what's going on, what the hell are you – "

"Relax, amigo," said Ramon as he got out of the car and went to the back seat to collect his hammocks. His brilliant teeth shone in the dark. "It doesn't pay for the gringos to know I can afford a car. Sell more hammocks this way."

They walked for five minutes and arrived at Joe's Cabanas. Lights twinkled over the tiki bar, but no one was there.

"Lively place you brought me to," sneered Pete, "you sure it's even open?"

"Si, si," nodded Ramon. "The lights wouldn't be on if it wasn't."

Pete sighed and took a seat on a bar stool. He surveyed the empty pool area, the empty-looking office, and was about to call out for some attention when Ramon put his fingers to his lips. He snuck behind the bar, picked up a rum bottle, and drank thirstily straight from it. Pete was about to do the same when he heard some noise from a nearby cabana. Ramon slipped back from behind the bar with the stealth of a cat and slid onto a stool, placing his precious hammocks beside him.

Joe emerged from Katrina's cabana, looked up and saw his guests. He scowled at Ramon, but was welcoming to Pete.

"Sorry for the wait, but I had to help put someone to bed. That first travel day'll kill ya." He looked skeptically at Ramon. "Found someone to buy you a drink, did you?" He gave a sarcastic chuckle. "Don't you have to hike back up to the mountains tonight?"

Ramon grinned, wiped a trickle of rum off his lip, and said, "Tonight, no, tonight I am — "

"Save it for the tourists," interrupted Joe, holding up a hand. He looked over Pete's tan, his filthy jeans and unkempt look. "Looks like you've been here for a while. Looking for a cabana for the night?"

Pete shrugged and said, "We'll see. First, I need a drink. Two cervezas for me and my friend."

"Your friend, huh?" said Joe sarcastically, but he fetched the beers.

Ramon nodded towards Katrina's cabana. "Some turista have too many drinks, Joe?"

Joe was about to reply when he heard a noise, looked up and saw Heidi struggling with Katrina's door. He put down the bar towel he was holding and went over to help her, saying over his shoulder, "Damn doors get stuck all the time. The humidity from the ocean warps 'em."

Pete watched Joe approach the cabana, and wondered if he had enough time to copy Ramon's trick. He reached over behind the bar, grabbed the rum bottle, and took a slug. He almost dropped it when the woman at the door of the cabana turned toward the bar as Joe wrestled with the door.

Quickly replacing the rum bottle, Pete whispered, "Holy shit."

Ramon, who'd been feeding the so-called guard dog some tortilla chips from a bowl on the bar, followed Pete's gaze. "Aiee! Muchacha! She wasn't here a couple of days ago."

Pete, his eyes still on Heidi, said, "Sounds like you keep your eye on the place." Ramon grunted. "I keep my eye on every place, you never know - "

"Never know what?" asked Pete, barely listening. Then Heidi sashayed up to the bar and the conversation was forgotten.

Heidi didn't normally sashay, but she was trying to cover up the fact that she was quite drunk. She'd put Katrina to bed after two pina coladas apiece, obviously very strong ones, and she was beginning to wonder if she should've done the same. No wonder she was feeling wobbly – even though she could hold her liquor, the only thing she'd eaten all day was that crappy sub on the plane.

So she sashayed up to the bar to cover her stagger, as the handsome Mexican man quickly moved his hammocks aside, and then she slumped down on the barstool between him and the gorgeous gringo beside him.

"Hello, boys," she said, feeling kind of Mae West. She glanced around the empty bar. "Feeling kind of lonely out here?"

"Not anymore," said the gringo with a grin, and the Mexican nodded happily and sidled up to her.

"Where's Joe?" asked Heidi, looking around. Then, seeing him return from Katrina's cabana, said, "Oops, I forgot."

"Forgot what?" asked the Mexican.

"He was helping me shut the door. Helping me put my friend to bed."

"Too many pina coladas?" asked the gringo.

"Too many everything," nodded Heidi, struggling to keep her head up.

Joe came back behind the bar and Heidi took his hand. "Thanks so much, Joe. Don't know what I'd do without you."

"Go thirsty," said Joe. "What would you like?"

"I think I've had enough pina coladas for now – how 'bout a Margarita?"

"If you're up for it."

"Damn right I am! This is my first night in Mexico! I can't go to bed yet!"

"Is your friend as beautiful as you?" asked the Mexican, who was damn cute, though a little short for Heidi's taste.

"She's a cow," giggled Heidi, sipping on her Pina Colada.

"I figured," said the gringo. "You hotties always have an ugly one tagging along for seconds, don't you?"

Heidi put her head down and laughed, nearly dipping her beautiful red hair in her frothy drink. She shook the men's hands. "I'm Heidi, and she's Katrina – though I don't think you'll be seeing her anytime soon."

They made introductions and started to chat. Somehow Heidi was picking up a second wind, with all this handsome testosterone around, and Pete, the gringo, was looking awfully good. His Bad Boy-ness just oozed out of him, as did his gift of gab and his charm. Ramon kept trying to cut in, but when Pete wouldn't give him a chance, he focused on the so-called guard dog and fed him tortilla chips whenever Joe wasn't looking.

Ramon finally managed to cut into Pete's story of being robbed in Zipolite. "You know, that's how you gringos get robbed, you come down here, get shit-faced, think you're safe, out of the big city and everything, then boom!" He smacked his hand on the bar. "That's when the thieves get you."

Pete, who'd been surreptitiously feeding the dog while Ramon spoke, looked up and said, "Sounds like you're talking from personal experience."

"Me?" said Ramon. "I've never been robbed in my life."

"I meant the other way around," said Pete.

Ramon shrugged. "Some people are so stupid they deserve to be robbed or have their rooms broken into."

Heidi, bored with this conversation, asked Joe if he had any food other than tortilla chips on offer.

"Sorry," said Joe. "We usually have better bar snacks at sunset happy hour, if you're around tomorrow."

Pete looked meaningfully toward Heidi, and said, "We might just be."

Joe, softened by Heidi's lovely face, said, "Maybe there's something I can grab out of the kitchen – maybe some dips to go with those chips."

"Chips?" said Heidi. She looked down at the empty bowl in front of her, as did Joe. He looked up at Pete in surprise. "Hey, that thing was full a few minutes ago."

Pete shrugged innocently. "I was hungry."

Joe looked at Ramon. "And you – "

Ramon shrugged. "Hey, my beer's paid for, no? I can have snacks if I want."

Joe leaned over the bar and looked at the dog, happily licking its chops and staring adoringly at both Pete and Ramon.

"Hmmph!" he said and stepped from the bar to go to the office and kitchen area. Heidi interrupted him. "Cute dog. What's his name?"

"Pecas. It's Spanish for 'freckles'."

Heidi glanced at the spotted dog. "Cute." As Joe left she said to the men, "He really seems to like you guys."

Pete and Ramon glared at each other, then Ramon said, "Hey, it's good to be friendly with the dog. You never know when it might attack."

"Yeah," said Pete, still glaring at Ramon. "You never know."

Joe returned from the office/kitchen and placed a bowl of chips and a couple of bowls of guacamole and salsa on the bar, pointedly in front of Heidi.

"Just be careful around here," he warned her, looking straight at Ramon, "there've been a few robberies along the beach lately."

Ramon shrugged. "Me, I'm just a poor hammock seller. I come down here from high up in the mountains, I must take two buses then walk for miles, I – "

Joe grunted and said, "Save it for the tourists, buddy." Then he looked up happily and said, "Here's some now," as a few people drifted rather drunkenly toward the bar.

As the customers sat down, Ramon reluctantly left Heidi and wandered over to them with his hammocks to do his shtick. By the time he returned, with no sales, and no chance of another free beer, Heidi and Pete were downright snuggly. Ramon snorted to himself, hefted his hammocks on his shoulder, and headed out for greener pastures.

Heidi, with some difficulty, got off her barstool and sashayed to the washroom. Pete and Joe watched her swaying form in admiration, and Joe said, "Last call. We're the last place to close on the beach, and that's at eleven. You want another drink? You want a cabana? I'm locking up for the night. You want to keep carryin' on after this, you have to go into town."

Pete, still watching Heidi, said, "I think I'm okay, thanks."

Joe snorted, said, "Good luck, amigo," and went over to the other customers to give last call.

After everyone else at the bar got their drinks to-go in plastic cups and headed to the beach, their cabanas, or started walking slowly toward town, Joe locked up the wooden slats over the bar and left Heidi and Pete sitting very close together. Joe said good-bye to Heidi, nice meeting her, since he probably wouldn't see her again, as he wouldn't be back from Puerto Vallarta until next Saturday.

Heidi, barely noticing him as she stared dreamily at Pete through squinty eyes, just nodded and shook his hand.

And then it was just them.

11   SCREWED

An odd shuffling sound woke up a very groggy Heidi. She peered into the semi-darkness to see a strange man sitting on her bed in his underwear. Only it wasn't a strange man, come to think of it. It was Pete, the man she'd met just a few hours ago at Joe's bar, the one she'd... Oh, shit! She sat up and turned on her bedside light, and there was Pete, rifling through her purse.

"What the hell do you think you're doing?" she asked in her most imperious voice, though she probably sounded like a distraught frog.

Pete turned innocently toward her. "What does it look like?

Heidi grunted and wiped a smudge of spittle from her mouth. "What are you -

some sort of gigolo?"

Pete laughed. "No, just broke."

"But you said you still had some money left after the robbery!"

Pete grinned and held up a wad of cash. "I have more now."

Heidi grabbed for her purse, but Pete held it over his head.

"Part of our deal – half now and half later."

Heidi gave him a blank look. Pete stared back at her for a moment before breaking into a laugh. "Seriously?"

Heidi managed to look angry and confused at the same time. Pete looked amused.

"You seriously don't remember? I thought you could hold your liquor a little better than that."

"I can hold my liquor just fine," snapped Heidi, getting onto her knees and grabbing again for her purse. "It's you I'm having problems with."

Pete grinned as if he'd just been complimented and dangled the purse an inch from Heidi's fingertips.

Heidi sighed and glared at him. "C'mon, I can see you being an asshole and taking my money. But at least leave me my purse. It's a Chanel, you know."

"Why would you bring something like this here?" asked Pete, fondling the supple leather. "You might as well put a sign on your forehead that says 'Rob Me'." He inspected the purse more closely. "So that's what they look like. Seems like a lot of money for nothing if you ask me."

"I didn't ask you," said Heidi, losing balance on the sagging bed. She gave up and slumped down beside Pete before she could fall down. Her thigh grazed against his and he put a hand on it.

"I think you did."

"Did what?" asked Heidi, slapping his overly-friendly hand off her thigh.

"Ask me to take you to bed. You knew exactly what you were doing the moment you sashayed up to the bar."

"I didn't sashay," huffed Heidi, "I was staggering, for Chrissakes."

Pete laughed. "Well, you've got an awfully nice swing of the hips with that stagger of yours. Face it, if it hadn't been me, it would've been Ramon."

"He's too short for me."

"I think you would've done a Mexican midget wrestler if I hadn't gotten there first."

Heidi snorted. "That doesn't say much for you, does it? You're a disgusting pig, a piece of shit, a —"

"Nice try," said Pete. "I remember some real sweet words you called me just a couple of hours ago." He edged closer to Heidi on the bed and she quickly squirmed away.

"God, I've got a headache," she groaned.

"So let's do it again," leered Pete, moving closer. "Maybe it'll help."

Heidi slid further away, till she was almost on the edge of the bed. "Like hell. Just leave me my purse and my credit cards and crawl back into whatever hole you crawled out of."

"Of course," said Pete, "it's my code of ethics. Cash only. It's too easy to get caught with credit cards."

Still gripping the wad of bills, he handed over her purse, as if offering a bouquet of flowers.

"What a gentleman," sneered Heidi.

"No, just a petty thief," corrected Pete. "Nothing to get worked up about." He leaned even closer. "Unless you want to."

Heidi tried to squirm away again, but she was on the edge of the bed now, and she lost her balance and rolled off the edge, butt-first, onto the tile floor. Pete leaned over and peered down.

"You okay?"

"Oh, I'm just great," said Heidi, hastily pulling up her panties, which had somehow displaced themselves during her fall. "Damn, that's a hard floor."

Pete offered her a hand up, but she ignored it. She sat where she was, hugging her purse to her chest.

"Suit yourself," said Pete. "But I'm surprised you're not more curious about the money I just took." He grinned wolfishly. "Or do you pay all your lovers?"

Heidi jumped up from the floor and lunged to hit him, but he backed away just in time. "Why would I have to pay anyone to sleep with me? Have you looked at me lately?"

Pete shrugged. "I have to say, you looked better earlier in the evening…but no, I don't suppose you'd have to open your purse for anybody. You sure did open your mouth, though. Booze really makes you talk, Heidi. You told me all about your thing for Bad Boys, your girlfriend Katrina…all sorts of interesting stuff."

Heidi stared at him warily. "What did I say about Katrina?"

Pete grinned. "Some of the fuzziness wearing off? You told me she came along with you at the last minute and you didn't really want her to. Said she's a goody two-shoes and you didn't want her looking down her nose at your…adventures." Pete saw that he had Heidi's attention and he leaned closer. "But then you got to thinking, hmm, having her here might not be so bad after all, you might be able to take advantage of the situation."

Heidi reddened and jerked away from Pete. "This is ridiculous. You're a thief and God-knows-what and I'm calling the cops." She rummaged in her purse for a moment but stopped in confusion. "Shit. How do I call the cops in Mexico?"

Pete laughed, and Heidi said, "Joe, then. I'll tell him how you're stealing from his guests. I'm sure he'll just love that. He'll probably tell everyone in town to stay clear of you." She smirked. "Maybe he'll even arrange a lynch mob." She went back to digging in her purse. "Where is that damn thing?"

"You mean this?" said Pete, picking up Heidi's pink phone from the floor beside him. Heidi looked surprised, then annoyed, and she lunged for the phone, but Pete held it behind his back. "Sorry to disappoint you, sweetheart, but you can't tell Joe. He left for Puerto Vallarta a few hours ago, right after he closed up the bar. Forgot that, too, did you?" Pete waved the money in his hand then looked smugly at Heidi. "Anyway, if anyone should be scared of Joe right now, it's you."

Heidi stood up from the floor with some difficulty and looked more confused than ever. "Why on earth would I be scared of that sweet man?"

Pete smiled in a way that made Heidi want to smack the grin right off his face, that is, if his face weren't so damn handsome. He turned toward the bedside table, where two forty-ounce bottles of alcohol stood, one of them a third empty, two glasses beside it.

"How about a drink?" he said coolly, placing Heidi's phone on the table beside him, out of her reach, then lazily pouring from the opened bottle of tequila. "It'll make you feel better, take the edge off."

"What are you up to now?" said Heidi, still standing beside the bed and eyeing her phone hungrily.

"Here," said Pete, and Heidi accepted the glass he offered in spite of her suspicions. He took a sip from his glass and leaned back on the bed against the pillow, in no hurry to budge, another shit-eating grin on his face. "Sure you don't want to get drunk again and go another round?"

Heidi wanted to lunge at his smug self, but she restrained herself. He held up the bottle of tequila and peered at it. "You know, this stuff isn't half bad."

Heidi glanced at the bottle for the first time as she sipped her drink. "If you say so," she said with a slight grimace. She was about to say something else when something niggled at her memory, and she looked back at the bottle with a strange sense of unease. She grabbed it from Pete's hand and studied it.

"Where did this come from?" she asked, her unease growing. "I didn't buy any duty-free on the plane." She took another sip and peered more closely at the label. "Shit, they don't even sell this on the plane."

Pete laughed. "Ah – the fog begins to lift!" He leaned forward and brushed a lock of hair out of Heidi's eye. "You stole it from Joe's bar – don't you remember?"

"What!" cried Heidi.

Pete held up Heidi's phone. "I've got it all right here. Took all the photos myself. Pretty impressive shots, if you ask me."

Heidi made another lunge for the phone, but Pete was too quick. "Give that back to me! Use your own damn phone!"

Pete shook his head in mock sadness. "I'd love to, but someone stole it in Zipolite when I was staying in that crappy hammock place. And when you left this little beauty just sitting on the bar last night – how could I resist?"

Heidi scowled at him but he just grinned back at her. "But that wasn't even the best part, Heidi. The best part was after that – when you decided you wanted to take your own pictures."

"Pictures of what?" said Heidi, a chill creeping up her back.

Pete leaned forward and smiled sweetly. "When your friend Katrina returns to the land of the living, you want to take pictures of her - with me - in a very compromising position."

He took a sip of his tequila and licked his lips. "Pictures you could send to Katrina's boyfriend, of course."

12   A DAY AT THE BEACH

Katrina woke up kind of fuzzy, wondering why it was so brutally bright. Had she left the curtains open? Why was there a small green lizard glued to the ceiling, staring down at her? And why did she hear roosters crowing so loudly that they were making her head pound?

A knock on the door made Katrina sit up, and the movement seemed to clear her mind. She suddenly remembered where she was and why, and she groaned. The knocking continued, and she shouted hoarsely, "Come in already!"

The door creaked, and with some shoving of the wood, Heidi stepped in, carrying two Styrofoam cups of coffee. She wore a demure sundress that was somehow still sexy, and she looked refreshed and wide awake. Katrina wanted to kill her.

"Chop-chop," said Heidi, staring at Katrina's dishevelment. "There's lots to do and only so much time."

"God," said Katrina, taking the coffee and gratefully sipping on it. "I thought this was a vacation."

"Sure it is, but I have to go to the bank machine before we go for breakfast, then we have to hit the beach and then – "

"Whoa," said Katrina, who was usually much livelier in the morning, but usually didn't drink so much the day before, either. "I thought we both went to the bank machine yesterday at the airport."

"Sure," said Heidi, looking strangely evasive. "But I went kind of crazy last night and bought rounds for everybody at the bar."

"I don't remember that," said Katrina.

"That's because Joe had to help me lug you into bed."

"Joe?"

"Joe the owner, the bartender," said Heidi impatiently. "We met him when we got here yesterday."

"Oh," said Katrina, vaguely remembering a big, burly guy behind the bar giving them pina coladas on the house. "Right. Joe." She blushed. "God, I didn't make a complete idiot of myself, did I?"

"Don't worry," said Heidi, "Joe and the dog and I were the only ones around to notice."

Katrina sighed with relief. "So how late did you stay up?"

Heidi seemed evasive again, focused on sipping her coffee. "Not that late."

"Meet anyone interesting?"

Heidi seemed to choke on her coffee, then recovered and said, "Not really."

Katrina gave her a strange look. Heidi was usually full of funny details and stories after a night out. But now she was unusually quiet. Oh, well, maybe she was just hungover. "Okay then, I'll just get dressed and find my purse and – "

"Keep an eye on it!" Heidi cut in, so quickly and urgently that Katrina turned to stare at her. She blushed a little, which Heidi rarely did, and Katrina looked at her curiously.

Heidi shrugged. "Just to be on the safe side. You never know."

Katrina nodded. "Okay. Why don't I meet you by the pool? I have to go to the bathroom before we leave."

"You haven't been throwing the paper in the toilet, have you?" said Heidi.

"Where else would I put it?"

"Oh God," said Heidi, rolling her eyes, back to her old self. "You don't know what the septic systems are like down here. You have to throw the paper in the waste basket."

"The waste basket?" said Katrina, horrified. "That's disgusting!"

"Not as disgusting as a clogged-up toilet. You have no idea what – "

"Okay, okay," said Katrina, cutting her off as quickly as she could. "I get the picture." She rummaged around and found her purse. "Where do they serve the breakfast here, anyway? I hope we're not too late. I didn't notice a dining room when we got here…not that I'd really remember anyway."

Heidi gave her a funny look. "Breakfast is anytime and anywhere you want, Dorothy. You're not in the compound anymore."

Katrina looked embarrassed. "Oh." She shrugged. "How am I supposed to know all this stuff? I've only been – "

Heidi softened. "I know, I know. I'm sorry, I'm being snotty. Well, a reverse snob, anyway. Look, I'll meet you out by the pool in a couple of minutes, okay? Then we'll find a nice place for breakfast — something without a huge lineup of fat people and a nasty-looking buffet."

They walked along the dirt road facing the beach, were thankful to find an ATM so they wouldn't have to go into town on their first day, peeked into the shop windows and then found a nice open-air place on the beach that was still serving breakfast, even though it was almost time for lunch. Afterwards Heidi bought a few cans of beer at a corner store, then they went back to change into their bikinis and hit the beach.

Heidi started laying down her towel a good distance from a nearby palapa beach bar, and Katrina said, "Hey, why don't we go sit over there? They've got lounge chairs."

"Because you have to drink there to get a chair, and we've already got beer."

"Oh," said Katrina. "But it'll be a lot more comfortable, and there's a bathroom."

"Probably not one you'd want to use," laughed Heidi. "We're not far from our place; you can always run up there. Or – " she waved at the vast expanse of ocean — "you've got a giant toilet right there."

"That's gross," said Katrina.

"Hey," said Heidi, taking off her sarong, "the fish do it."

Katrina gazed at Heidi's tiny bikini. "Look at you. You've got a tan already and no tan lines by the look of things."

"Travel agency perk," said Heidi, making her sarong into a pillow and lying back. "One of my clients owns a tanning salon and gives me freebies."

"And free melanoma."

Heidi shrugged. "So I'll die pretty." She glanced over at Katrina, who was shyly pulling her beach cover-up over her head. "I hope you put on plenty of lotion. Looks like you haven't been in the sun in a while."

"Heidi, it's February. What do you expect?"

"Oh yeah," said Heidi. "Hard to remember when you're down here in this heat." She sat up and pulled two beers from a plastic bag, which she'd filled with ice.

"Here."

Katrina accepted the can and said, "I don't know if I should be having this, after yesterday. But you know, it's weird, I feel amazingly good, just a bit of a headache."

"Yeah," said Heidi, popping open her can of Pacifico. "It's something about the latitude or longitude or something, but the farther south I go, the less hungover I get."

Katrina took a sip of her beer. "Maybe it's just being drunk all the time when you're down here."

Heidi nodded. "That could be it."

"Oh look!" said Katrina excitedly. "Horses!"

"Yeah," said Heidi, who was getting into suntan position. "They have those down here, too."

"Oh my God," said Katrina, forcing Heidi to sit up.

"What?"

"Look!"

A Mexican cowboy, riding alongside a tourist, stopped and dismounted. The horse took a huge dump in the sand as the tourist, oblivious, awkwardly dismounted as well. The cowboy leaned behind the horse, pulled a plastic bag from his pocket, and, with his bare hands, placed the shit in the bag. He wiped his hands in the sand, then on his pants, and asked the unsuspecting tourist for his fee. The tourist handed over the money, they shook hands, and the cowboy shuffled in the sand back in the other direction, looking for more customers.

"Oh God!" said Katrina. "I hope he's not the guy who cooked my breakfast."

Heidi was rolled over laughing. "Now that, Katrina, is the real Mexico!"

Heidi had brought along a tiny Ipod/stereo system, very retro these days, but that was what she liked about it. And she was glad she'd brought it, since Pete had commandeered her phone. But the combination of that, the music playing in the nearby palapa, and the mariachis strolling along the beach serenading sunbathers was too much. After a while she gave up.

And all the music in the world couldn't distract her from the thoughts whirling in her head.

Her first thought was guilt: she'd pimped Katrina out to Pete.

As far as she could recall – and it was all a bit of a blur, with some bits and pieces remembered by her, and supplemented very happily last night by Pete – it had all started innocently enough.

She'd told Pete that her girlfriend Katrina was in a lousy relationship and deserved better. Katrina was on the fence about the whole thing and just needed a little nudge to see that there were other men out there, men more interesting and - to flatter Pete - far more attractive. Maybe if Pete just flirted with Katrina a little bit, she'd get the uplift she needed, feel better about herself, and dump Tate.

But Pete had said, "Why stop there? If you really want your friend to dump this guy so you can have him for yourself –
"

Heidi had been quick to cut in. "I never said – "

"Oh, it's pretty obvious, don't you think?" said Pete. "You want this Tate guy for yourself. Otherwise, why sic me on Katrina?" He'd grinned then. "I'm perfectly willing to go a lot further than flirtation – for a price."

And that was where it had become fuzzier for Heidi – whether from guilt or tequila, she wasn't sure – and Pete had filled her in on the remaining events:

"I said, why not take a picture of me making out with Katrina and send it to her beloved Tate. That ought to take care of things. And you just jumped all over that idea, Princess."

"Don't call me Princess," Heidi had quickly said. "Tate calls me that."

"It seems fitting," said Pete. "Anyway, Princess, you liked that idea so much you offered to pay me half now and half later – after the deed was done. And I said, throw in a couple of nice meals and I'm good to go."

And Heidi, sipping tequila with Pete on the bed post-coitus, had groaned and looked at him with disbelief. "You're making this up. I haven't always been the sweetest kid on the block, but I'd never – "

"Oh yes, you would," and Pete's smile had made her cringe.

"You're just saying all this to get money out of me," said Heidi, still holding onto a shred of hope that she hadn't been as nasty and devious as Pete claimed. "And besides, I'm relatively sober now and I think you're full of shit and I've changed my mind about the whole thing." She held out her hand. "So give me my money and my phone back."

Pete shook his head. "I was afraid you might pull something like this – so I got myself some collateral."

And that was when he showed Heidi the photos of her he'd taken with her phone.

Heidi looked over at Katrina now, who was too excited to lie down on her blanket, sitting up, basking in the sights and sounds around her. An innocent little lamb about to be led to slaughter…Heidi had really never intended it to go this far. A little flirtation, sure. But not this. Sure, she would've liked to see Kat flirt with Pete – or, preferably, anyone else but Pete – but in the cold (well, very hot, actually) light of day she was regretting the whole thing – she was fond of Kat, after all – and even though she was furious with Pete for what he'd done, she still found him incredibly hot. That damn Bad Boy thing – she just couldn't get away from it.

Katrina was too nice and naïve to deal with a rat like Pete. Before Heidi had booted Pete out of her room last night, she'd even tried to change his mind by telling him how unattractive Katrina was, that he'd really lose interest in her if he saw her. He hadn't been deterred in the least. So it would be less of a challenge, he said. A deal was a deal.

"No – blackmail is blackmail," said Heidi.

Those damn pictures. Pete had giggled like a little boy when he showed them to Heidi. Apparently, once everyone was gone from the bar, they had necked and talked, talked and necked. Heidi blabbing away about Katrina and Tate, Pete listening intently, goading her on. When she finally shut up and took her lips away from Pete's long enough to breathe, she realized their drinks were gone and she was awfully thirsty.

"I know how you can fix that," said Pete.

"How?" said Heidi, leaning into him, nearly knocking them both off their stools.

Pete grinned slyly and pointed to the wooden slats over the bar.

"See that padlock there?"

Heidi squinted and he adjusted her head a little, to look in the right direction.

"I watched Joe when he locked that up. Thing is, he was in such a hurry to get on the road, he didn't close it properly. If you look really close, you'll see it."

Heidi squinted a little more and sure enough, the padlock wasn't fully latched.

"All you have to do," said Pete, "is go in there and open it up, and you can drink whatever you want."

Heidi looked around doubtfully. "What about that giant spotlight shining right on the bar?"

Pete shrugged. "To keep the thieves away from here at night. But look around – there's nobody here, no one on the street, no one's going to see you."

"Me?" squealed Heidi.

"You're the thirsty one," said Pete. "It was your idea."

Heidi giggled. "I suppose it was, wasn't it?"

She straightened up, almost sober for a moment. "But what about their inventory?"

Pete laughed. "In this place?"

"Cameras?"

"In this place?"

"What about the dog?" Heidi persisted, and looked around. "Where's the dog? He might bark at us."

"Pecas the guard dog is full of tortilla chips and sleeping right under your feet."

Heidi looked down at the furry mound beside her bar stool. "Oh."

Pete snuggled even closer. "You are thirsty, aren't you?"

Heidi giggled again. "Sure am." She took a deep breath. "Well...okay."

She slid off her bar stool, managed to stay upright, checked the pool and the grounds, then snuck around behind the bar. She reached up to the padlock, unlatched it and slid open the wooden doors.

"Smile!" said Pete, as he focused Heidi's phone on her.

Heidi turned and stuck her tongue out at him, then turned back to the bar and reached for a half-full bottle of tequila, changed her mind, and grabbed a full one. She placed it on the bar in front of Pete, then thought a second and went back to the bar and grabbed a bottle of rum. She placed that beside the tequila on the bar and Pete gave her a thumbs-up.

Enjoying the attention, all thoughts of sobriety gone, Heidi grinned, shook her hips, and, to top it all off, so to speak – slid her dress down over her shoulders, gave a big tug – and flashed her boobs.

Heidi had played many stupid drunken pranks over the years – a major mooning at a high-class wedding came to mind – but she'd never been blackmailed over one before. And there she was, post-romp, sitting in the bed beside Pete, sipping tequila and pleading with him to forget the whole thing.

"A deal's a deal," repeated Pete, enjoying her squirm. "You give me the money you promised me, I do the deal I promised you, or else I get Joe's e-mail and send him these tasty tidbits. I don't think he'd be too happy with you. Not just for the stealing, but, you know, the principle of it and all. He'd probably kick you out."

"He's out of town," protested Heidi. "He might not even check his e-mail."

Pete shrugged. "The other bartender might like to see my little slideshow. Him, or whoever runs the office."

Heidi thought of sweet little Teresa, who'd checked them into their rooms, no doubt sweet little uptight Catholic Teresa, and shuddered.

"They can't kick me out. I already paid in full so I'd get a discount. It's non-refundable."

Pete seemed unconcerned with her problem. "You told me about your inheritance; you don't have to worry about the money. So go stay somewhere else."

"And how do I explain that to Katrina?"

Pete finished his tequila and stood up, cramming Heidi's money into his pants pocket. "That's your problem, sweetheart, isn't it?"

He started to place the phone in his shirt pocket, and Heidi grabbed his arm. "C'mon, Pete, give me back the phone." He shook his head. She said, "Just take the memory card then, and leave the phone."

"I lost my phone in Zipolite, remember? I could use one for a few days. I promise I'll give it back when I leave. Pink's really not my colour."

Heidi snarled. "I use that thing for everything! Seriously, how am I supposed to live without my phone?"

Pete laughed. "You were born without it, weren't you?"

Heidi tried to keep her anger in check. "And how exactly am I supposed to get the incriminating photos of you and Katrina when you've got the phone? Follow the two of you around like a frisky puppy?"

Pete laughed. "You? More like a rabid dog. But don't worry – I'll know when the time's right and I'll slip the phone to you beforehand."

"Sounds like a brilliant plan," scoffed Heidi.

"Hey, it was your plan, Princess." Pete waggled the phone at her. "I just changed it up a bit. And when the deed is done, you'll get your pretty pink phone back, good as new. Everything you want, you get. Exactly as promised."

Heidi sat up on her beach towel, thinking of the smug sneer on Pete's face as he'd left her room last night, and pulled her watch from her purse. Time was running out. She and Katrina were supposed to 'accidentally' meet Pete, presumably a total stranger, at Joe's bar around three this afternoon.

"Katrina," she said, looking at her friend who was staring, enraptured, out at the waves. "You remember what I said to you at the bar last night?"

Katrina turned to her and scoffed. "Are you crazy?"

Heidi was affronted. "I didn't think it was that bad an idea."

"I mean you're crazy to even think I could remember anything about when we got here." Katrina turned to stare at Heidi. "What was a bad idea?"

Heidi averted her gaze and nonchalantly stirred her fingers in the sand. "Well, I said I thought you needed a man, at least needed to flirt with a man, to lift your spirits, feel more desirable after the whole Tate bullshit."

"Oh God," said Katrina, rolling her eyes. "What have you done? You're not setting me up with someone, are you?"

"Of course not," said Heidi quickly, "it's just..."

"Just what?" asked Katrina suspiciously.

Heidi continued to avoid Katrina's eyes. "Well, I'd like to see you flirt and have a little fun, but just remember to be careful, okay?"

Katrina frowned. "Since when did you turn into my mother? First, it's my purse, now it's the men..." She finished her beer and threw it into the plastic bag with the other empties. "It's hard enough to figure out what to do about Tate, without you complicating things by trying to get me to hang out with other guys." Now it was Katrina's turn to avert her gaze and sift sand through her fingers. "Who knows, maybe I do love Tate."

"After he forgot your birthday? After he didn't even call you after your argument?"

"My battery was dead."

"I don't remember seeing any messages on the phone at your apartment when we were there."

Katrina snorted. "As if I'd remember."

"Well, I would," said Heidi, "and there weren't." Heidi stared thoughtfully at Katrina. Maybe there was a way to turn this thing around. Take a picture of Pete kissing Katrina – no biggie, but it would look big to Tate – then interrupt them before things got too steamy. There! The best of both worlds! Tate would break up with Katrina, and she'd still have Pete all to herself. And after Pete was history – she'd have Tate, too.

Heidi took a deep breath and said, almost lightly, "I'm just saying, maybe The Great Upheaval isn't such a bad thing. Maybe you should be thinking things over. Maybe the psychic was right. Maybe you should be on the lookout for a tall, dark, handsome stranger."

"Oh, Heidi – seriously?"

"Just sayin'."

Katrina finally looked at her and shrugged. "I don't know…I just don't know." Suddenly she jumped up and brushed the sand off her legs. "Anyway, the hell with it all right now. I'm going for a swim."

13 SLAM-DUNKED

Heidi jumped up and pointed at the large breakers. "In that? Are you insane? It's dangerous out there, Kat. Just look at the people trying to get in and out of the water. The only one who's making it look easy is that girl who swims like a seal. Must be a mermaid – or from Hawaii." Katrina was starting for the shore. Heidi called out after her. "I hear there's a calmer beach not far away! We can go there tomorrow if you want!"

Katrina had been watching the breakers for a while, fascinated by the way the waves crashed so close to shore. Obviously, this made getting in and out very difficult: those who tried getting in usually got knocked down or whipped back to shore, and those trying to get out, who made it almost back to dry land, got knocked down by a wave and sucked back out again.

But Katrina was determined. If all those other people could at least try it, so could she. She turned back to Heidi. "You're right – it's not the Caribbean. But I have to at least try it while I'm here. It would make Kevin proud. He's always telling me I should try new things."

Heidi snorted. "He won't be proud of you if you're dead. Hey – this isn't some sort of kamikaze mission, is it?"

Alarmed now, Heidi strode (as quickly as you can stride in sand) after her. "Okay, but I'm coming with you – and stay close to shore."

Katrina took a deep breath and stuck her toes in the water. Then she stepped in. The soft wet sand felt like silk under her feet. But she could already feel the water trying to tug her in as a wave crashed just inches away from her. The sand sank down, her toes with it. Katrina took an automatic step back, then another deep breath, and another step forward.

Heidi, just a couple of metres behind Katrina, was distracted by someone calling to her. The mariachi band had finally made their way to them, and the men, in their clean and starched white outfits, started serenading her. Heidi tried waving them away, then pointed at Katrina, and made a swimming motion. The mariachis stopped playing and watched with amusement as Heidi ran to the shoreline and started in after Katrina. A few Mexican children who'd been playing nearby followed the gaze of the mariachis and went over to join them in the entertainment.

Heidi waded out only knee-deep, and she could already feel a drag as the waves receded. She shouted to Katrina, who was a couple of metres away. She looked nervous but excited. She saw a wave coming and turned her back to it so she wouldn't get slammed too hard.

Heidi yelled, "Look out!" The wave looked huge, looming behind Katrina's head, and Heidi winced and took a few awkward steps back, barely staying on her feet.

But it was too late. Katrina got smashed by the incoming wave and thrown down under it. She'd just managed to gain her footing and get up again when another wave came booming down on her. Heidi tried to make her way toward her, but the waves kept pushing her back.

Suddenly a man ran toward them, dove unhesitatingly into the water like a seasoned lifeguard, and hauled a sputtering Katrina back to shore. He dragged her safely away from the waves, coughing and shaking, and the Mexicans stared avidly, as if watching a floundering fish, ready to take a poke at it.

When it was clear Katrina was going to survive, the mariachis started playing happily, and the kids giggled at Katrina's sagging bottoms and her bikini top, which was very close to falling off. But after a few minutes, with no more action, they trailed off, disappointed – the show was over.

Heidi somehow managed to scramble out of the water, and, breathless, she started toward Katrina. But Katrina waved her away, then suddenly puked up a bucketful of sea water and beer.

The mariachis surrounded them and played very loudly, and one of them held out his hand for a tip. Heidi scowled at them till they shrugged and strolled away. As she watched them go, the man who'd rescued Katrina approached them.

Heidi gaped. "Where the hell did you come from?" She glanced over at Katrina, who was bent over and hacking too loudly to hear.

Pete grinned and held out his hands. "Lucky break, huh?"

Heidi continued to stare at him. Pete nodded at the nearby palapa bar.

"I was having a drink and watching the waves when…" He shrugged innocently.

Heidi hissed at him. "That wasn't our plan."

Pete shrugged again and wiped salt water from his eyes. "Just good timing. And I figured some heroics would help things along."

"That's cheating. You're just supposed to have sex with her, not make her fall for you."

"Well, she kind of did," laughed Pete. "Literally."

"Look," said Heidi, sidling closer to him. "I was thinking…I don't think you really have to…you know, go all the way…"

"All the way?" laughed Pete. "What is this, high school?"

Heidi ignored him. "I mean, you could…I could…you could just kiss her and I could take a photo and send it to Tate…I think that would be enough to seal the deal."

"Are you kidding?" laughed Pete. He nodded toward Katrina, who was still bent over, hacking. "You didn't tell me your friend was so cute. In fact, you kind of implied–" He made a barking sound and then grinned. "This is getting more fun by the minute. And a deal's a deal." He rudely pushed past a seething Heidi and walked over to Katrina, who'd finally stopped coughing and puking and was standing up almost straight.

He put an arm around her shoulder, and she didn't push it away. "How are you doing? Better now?"

Katrina stared up at him, caught her breath, and quickly turned from blue to red. "Yeah," she murmured. "Better."

Heidi stared at Pete. Damn, he was gorgeous, even with his dark hair dripping wet and his eyes watering. What had she done? She'd practically offered him up Katrina on a platter – and now she realized, in spite of him being a cocky bastard and a petty thief, and maybe even because of it – that she wanted him for herself.

He was looking at Katrina with tender concern. "You could probably use a drink."

Katrina laughed feebly. "Well, I think all my bodily fluids are gone by now."

Heidi, finding herself unreasonably jealous, looked over Katrina and said, "And you could probably use that shower by the pool. You've got droopy-drawers, big-time."

Katrina glanced down, horrified, at her bulging bottoms, which appeared to be holding at least a kilo of sand. She turned even redder.

Pete laughed and squeezed Katrina's shoulder. "Happens to the best of us." He started helping Katrina to collect her things, ignoring Heidi's.

"C'mon," he said, "Let's go up to Joe's bar and have ourselves a cocktail."

"Yeah," said Heidi sarcastically, glaring at him as she picked up her things. "Why on earth didn't I think of that? That sounds like a brilliant plan."

14 DROOPY-DRAWERS

As they approached the bar, Katrina in her swimsuit cover-up to hide her droopy-drawers, and Heidi nonchalantly strutting in her bikini, Pecas the spotted dog came running to greet Pete, happily wagging his tail.

"Hey, Pecas," said Pete, patting the dog. "How ya doin'?

"How do you know the dog?" asked Katrina.

Pete, catching himself, said, "Oh, I booked a cabana here earlier and had a drink." He gave Heidi a wink, then turned to shake Katrina's hand. "By the way, I'm Pete."

"I'm Katrina, and this is my friend Heidi. We got in last night."

"Oh, you're staying here?" said Pete innocently.

"For a week," said Katrina. "If I don't drown myself before that. Thanks a lot for helping me back there."

"Hey," said Pete with a grin, "what are new friends for?"

Pete took a seat at the bar and ushered the girls to do the same. Heidi glanced quickly at the bartender, then turned her back to him. She looked sidelong at Pete, who smiled back innocently while he made a phoning motion with his thumb and little finger. Katrina stood uncomfortably beside Heidi for a minute, shifting from one foot to the other with a grimace. Then she said, "I'd better go shower off in my room."

"Are you kidding?" said Heidi. "And leave a sandy mess all over the floor? That'll clog the drain for sure."

Katrina groaned and said, "Maybe the pool?"

Pete pointed to a sign by the pool that read NO SAND OR SURFBOARDS IN THE POOL.

"Okay," said Katrina, "I can understand the sand bit— but surfboards?"

"Guess the surfers get pretty wild around here," said Pete, thinking how cute Katrina's discomfort was.

Heidi chirped in, "Use the outdoor shower. Just take off that cover-up, put your towel around you, then dump out the sand and adjust everything down there. No one will be the wiser."

Katrina looked at the pool, where several people were swimming, or lounging on chairs, beer cans and cigarettes in hand. The shower was just to the right of the pool, in full view of everyone.

Pete, sensing her distress, said, "How about a quick drink first? It'll make it easier for you."

"Yeah," said Katrina, "I think a drink's a great idea – if my bottoms stay up long enough."

Pete laughed and turned to the bartender. Katrina stared at him. He was tall and lanky and pale.

"Hey, you're not the guy who was here last night."

"No," said the bartender, "I'm Craig. Joe's gone up to Puerto Vallarta to see some friends for the week."

Heidi took a deep breath and finally turned around. "I'm Heidi," she pronounced, as if expecting a reaction. Craig stared at her blankly.

"Do I know you?" he said, colouring a little, wondering how he could've forgotten a girl who looked like that.

Heidi blushed too, and glanced at Pete, who'd taken a sudden interest in Pecas at his feet.

"Oh no, no!" she said, "I just didn't…I thought…I thought you looked like someone I know."

"I get that a lot," said Craig. And then, with chagrin, "Usually like somebody's kid brother."

"Well it's nice to meet you," said Heidi, obviously relieved, and aware of Pete's snicker beside her. "Heidi and Katrina. We're here for a week. I think you'll get to know us."

"I sure hope so," said Craig with a smile, then, "What can I get you guys?"

Pete ordered a round of margaritas, giving Heidi a knowing look, and she glared at him, but he ignored her.

"Just be careful," said Pete, as he watched Katrina pick up her cocktail. "Tequila can make people talk."

"I've got nothing to hide," said Katrina, drinking very fast.

"Good for you," said Pete, glancing at Heidi. "Not everyone can say that – especially in Mexico."

"Why's that?" said Katrina, licking the salt off the rim of her plastic glass. "Is this like Las Vegas or something? What happens in Mexico – "

"Stays in Mexico. Exactly!" And Pete toasted the girls. Craig looked on, amused, until a couple of burnt (in more ways than one) people walked up to the bar, and he turned to greet them.

"Okay," said Katrina, downing her drink. "There's no time like the present."

"For what?" said Heidi, so relieved at Craig's ignorance of her previous evening's shenanigans that she'd forgotten the whole droopy-drawers incident.

"For a shower," said Katrina, and she quickly took off her cover-up, grabbed her towel from her bag, and wrapped it around her. She strode to the pool with the same determination she'd strode to the ocean, and after a few seconds of figuring out the hot/cold taps, turned them on full-speed.

Full speed might have been too much. The water gushed out like a torrential downpour and she was soaked in seconds, towel included. She tried fiddling around with her bottoms to let the sand escape, one hand on the bottoms, the other clutching her towel, but it was too wet and heavy and fell down to her feet.

Katrina was caught there, her hand up the ass of her bottoms, the other hand tugging at her top, and someone by the pool noticed and pointed it out. Before Katrina knew it, everyone was pointing and laughing, enjoying the spectacle.

Katrina, mortified, gave up on dumping the whole sandy load, adjusted her top and bottoms, threw aside the towel, then dove into the pool, staying underwater as long as she could. When she was out of breath, she finally emerged and was greeted by the applause of all the onlookers. With the tequila from the margarita having sunk in, she sputtered, shook her hair, and swam to the ladder. She gave a bow, took a deep breath, jogged over to pick up her towel, then walked as proudly as she could back to the bar.

Heidi, Pete, and Craig clapped as she slid onto a stool.

"Now that was a performance!" said Pete. "Though I could've helped you out at the shower if you'd wanted."

Katrina smacked his arm playfully, and gratefully picked up the new margarita that awaited her. "I think I'm done with performances for the day – maybe for the week."

"Oh, performances are fun," said Pete with a leer. "Aren't they, Heidi?"

"Depends on who sees them, I guess," said Heidi, gulping down half her drink as she glared at Pete.

"Well it looks like everybody here saw mine," said Katrina, gulping her drink down, too.

At this rate, thought Pete, it's going to be a very early siesta.

Sensing this wasn't the time to make a move, he started talking to a couple of other tourists at the bar. Katrina tipsily nudged Heidi and nodded toward Pete.

"Tall, dark, and handsome. How random is that? Just like the psychic said."

Heidi snorted. "I don't know about the handsome part."

"Are you serious?" said Katrina. "He's gorgeous."

"If you like that type," said Heidi. "Looks like a definite Bad Boy to me. No longer my type, remember?"

"Oh," said Katrina, "Bronwyn. Right. I wonder how long that's going to last."

"What's that supposed to mean?" said Heidi, only half pretending to be deeply offended.

"Oh come on, Heidi, I know you're here to pick up men, that's part of the reason you didn't want me tagging along. Don't let me cramp your style."

"I'm starting to wonder if I might be cramping yours," said Heidi as she looked at Pete flirting outrageously with a girl who was obviously at the bar with her boyfriend. "You seem awfully hot for this guy. What, you forget about dear old Tate all of a sudden?"

"You're the one who told me to forget about him for a week," reminded Katrina.

Heidi was about to respond when Craig came over with a basket of tortilla chips and a bowl of some strange-looking food.

"Ceviche," he said, "give it a try. It's delicious."

"What on earth is that?" said Katrina, wrinkling her nose and temporarily forgetting Heidi's words.

"Fish and seafood cooked in lime juice," replied Craig.

Katrina stared at the bowl. "You mean it's raw?"

"No," said Craig, amused. "The acid in the lime juice cooks it, breaks down the membranes or something. Just try it."

"It's fabulous, believe me," said Heidi. "I've had it lots of times."

"Then you try it," said Katrina.

"No thanks," said Heidi, "I'm saving myself for dinner."

Katrina cautiously picked up the bowl, sniffed it, and immediately handed it back to Craig. "It smells weird. Is it supposed to smell like that?"

Craig laughed. "Hey, you're in Mexico, you're supposed to try new things!" He took a spoon from behind the bar and shovelled some into his mouth. He made a funny face, but Katrina wasn't sure whether it was because of the taste or whether he was making fun of her. She and Heidi laughed.

"No thanks," said Katrina, "but I'll take some chips and salsa if you've got any."

Craig handed over the snacks, and Pete's companions drifted over to the pool. He plunked himself down next to Katrina and ordered a beer.

"So," said Katrina, licking salsa off her lips, "What cabana are you in?"

"What – are you planning on sneaking in in the middle of the night?" asked Pete with a grin.

Katrina turned bright red and said, "Of course not! I was just making conversation."

117

Pete leaned closer. "I'm happy to make conversation with you, darlin', any time you want."

Heidi quickly cut in, leaning in between them. "How long are you planning on staying?" she asked.

"Maybe a week, maybe longer," said Pete, sipping his beer. "Depends what's going on, I guess."

"What do you mean?" asked Katrina.

Pete cleared his throat. "Well, I'm a housepainter back in Toronto, and if I can get any jobs here, I take them. It helps me pay my way. I've been here since November, started up in Mazatlan, went down to Huatulco, and now I'm heading my way back north, checking out the spots I missed on my way down."

"You don't look like a housepainter to me," mused Katrina. "More like….I don't know…maybe a bartender."

Pete laughed. "I used to be, but I got sick of dealing with people. I like houses better – they whine a lot less."

They heard a friendly bark from the dog, Pecas, and turned to see Ramon strolling toward the bar, hammocks in hand.

"Hey, amigos, how you feeling today?" He kissed Heidi on the cheek, then turned to Katrina. "So, you are the sick girlfriend, no? I had no idea you were so beautiful." And he kissed her on the cheek as well.

Katrina, taken aback, turned to Heidi. "You know this guy?"

Heidi turned away from Ramon, uncomfortable. "We might've met last night."

Ramon was affronted. "Might've? Might've? You, the love of my life, you forget me already?"

He put his hammocks on a nearby stool and made a swooning motion. Katrina laughed and arched an eyebrow at Heidi. "And you said you didn't meet anyone interesting."

Pete and Heidi exchanged knowing looks, and Ramon turned to Pete and put a hand on his shoulder. "Hey, buddy, how 'bout a beer?"

Pete shrugged off Ramon's hand. Sneering, he stared pointedly in Ramon's eyes and said, "Do I know you?"

Ramon looked at Pete a moment, then Heidi and Katrina, then shrugged and said, "Ah, you know how it is – to me all you gringos look alike. Guess I thought you were someone else."

Ramon lifted the hammocks from the bar stool and thrust them toward Heidi and Katrina. "Me, I am Ramon, a poor hammock seller. I bring them every day from high up in the mountains, my family is very poor, I must take two buses and walk five miles each way every day."

Heidi laughed in spite of herself and said, "Sure, I remember you now, Ramon – I heard that same spiel last night."

Ramon looked offended. "It is no spiel, senorita. It is the real deal."

Katrina joined in Heidi's laughter, and Ramon looked at Pete, who was eyeing him warily, and said, "Crazy gringas, no?" Then, making sure Heidi and Katrina weren't looking, he made a smoking motion with his fingers to his lips and nodded toward the bathrooms. He slid off his stool, leaving his hammocks behind, and Pete waited a moment, then followed.

15 SMOKING IN THE BOYS' ROOM

Pete made sure the girls weren't looking, then slipped into the men's room after Ramon. He'd already lit a huge spliff, and was leaning against the sink.

"So, amigo," said Ramon with a lazy smile. "Que pasa?"

Pete squeezed himself into the tiny bathroom. "You couldn't have picked someplace bigger?"

"I did not know if you had a cabana yet."

"Got one this morning," said Pete with a frown. "No freebies for me."

"So, you didn't spend the night with the senorita?"

"She kicked me out."

Ramon laughed. "Didn't like what you had to give, eh?"

"Look," said Pete, irritated, but not irritated enough to refuse the joint that Ramon passed him. "You're not supposed to know me, or that I was with Heidi last night. Heidi and I, we made this deal – "

"Ah, so that's how it is," said Ramon, taking the joint back from Pete. "You know, I came back last night, hoping to sneak into her place and maybe lighten her purse just a little. And what did I see? You, leaving her cabana with your pockets much heavier than they were before."

"So?" said Pete warily.

"So, you're on my turf, man. And why am I not supposed to know that you have already been so friendly with Heidi?"

Pete remained silent, and took the joint back from Ramon, who watched him curiously, waiting for an answer.

Katrina, her bladder full of margaritas, left her stool to go to the bathroom by the pool.

"Why don't you just go to your cabana?" asked Heidi. "It's probably a lot cleaner."

"It's farther away," said Katrina, rushing toward the ladies' room.

She'd just finished wiping off the toilet seat, which apparently no one used, preferring to squat for target practice, when she heard voices coming through the open space between the ceiling and the wall next door to her.

Ramon finished off the joint, tossed it in the toilet, and looked squarely at Pete. "So you won't tell me what this deal of yours is?"

"And have you cut in on the action?" said Pete. "Not a chance, amigo."

"Well," said Ramon, "I have to make something out of all this." He pulled a baggie out of his pants pocket. "Buy some of this shit from me, amigo."

Pete handled the baggie, smelled it, and said, "I'd love to, man, but I'm kinda broke."

"I don't think so," said Ramon. He leaned closer to Pete.

Short though he was, he was threatening in the tiny bathroom.

"You know, you kinda owe me."

"I bought you a beer last night!" protested Pete.

"You know what I mean," said Ramon with a sneer. "Silence is golden."

"Okay," sighed Pete, taking out some money. "I'll buy twenty bucks' worth."

Ramon measured out the pot, grabbed some toilet paper and wrapped it inside, then handed it to Pete. Pete said, "Anyway, amigo, don't worry about your turf. I just have to do one quick job, then I'll be blowing town in a couple of days and you'll have the place to yourself."

Katrina, her ear to the wall, was confused. She recognized the voices as those of Pete and Ramon, but why had Pete told her he'd just arrived this morning, if he'd been here last night? And why had he pretended not to know Ramon? And she was sure, through her margarita-soaked mind, that Pete had said he'd be staying in town at least a week, though he was now saying he was leaving in a couple of days. And what was the job he was talking about? What on earth was going on with this guy?

Ramon, somewhat mollified, said, "Okay, enough about that for now." He smiled at Pete. "So, if you got tossed out, where did you spend the night?"

"On one of the lounge chairs by the pool," said Pete. "That ferocious guard dog didn't seem to mind."

Ramon laughed. "Good old Pecas." His voice became solemn. "You should be careful doing things like that, you know. You could be robbed blind."

Slightly stoned now, Pete looked at Ramon, and they both broke into helpless giggles.

Katrina, leaning toward the wall of the bathroom, trying to hear more of the conversation, was suddenly dissuaded from her mission by the sight of a flying cockroach the size of a small missile. Stifling a scream, she ran out of the ladies' room and straight to the bar, still waving her hands in front of her in self-defence.

Heidi, watching her friend tearing toward the bar as if in the midst of a murderous wasp infestation, said, "What's wrong, Kat?"

Katrina was breathing hard, her face red. God, she thought, how do I always get involved in these things? Were Pete and Ramon dope smugglers? It reminded her all again of Life of the Party and the time she'd been at Randy's house with his giant stash of cocaine.

Katrina gasped, "A big bug. A really, really big bug. I'm going to go use the washroom in my cabana."

"Probably won't be any better," said Heidi, "unless you hole up in your mosquito netting."

"Look, I really have to talk to you when I get back," said Katrina over her shoulder as she dashed toward her cabana.

Craig leaned toward Heidi, feigning deep thought. "Hmm. Mosquito netting. Not a bad idea. You could have a great party in there."

Heidi smiled teasingly. "I think that might lead to a lot of entanglements."

"Just what I was thinking," said Craig with a wink, but then somebody across the bar called his name and he hurried over.

Pete and Ramon sauntered back to the bar, slightly squinty-eyed, and asked where Katrina had gone.

"To her cabana to pee," said Heidi. "She tried the public washrooms but they didn't work out so well for her."

"The public washrooms?" said Pete, slightly alarmed.

"I'm sure they're not that bad," said Heidi. "God knows I've seen a lot of them in my travels."

Pete gave Ramon a look, and he shrugged, and Pete looked anxiously toward Katrina's cabana, wondering what she'd overheard.

Ramon, taking advantage of the moment, snuggled up to Heidi and whispered in her ear. "You know, I think something very strange is going on here, but I don't know what."

"Oh?" said Heidi innocently.

"Oh yes," said Ramon, caressing her arm. "And I'm sure I'll find out sooner or later."

Heidi nudged him away and said, "Well let me know when you do," and tried to turn back to Pete, but Ramon wouldn't let her. He turned his back to Pete and lowered his voice.

"I know that you and Pete don't want Katrina to know you were together last night."

Heidi shrugged. "Katrina doesn't approve of things like that."

"What else doesn't she approve of?" asked Ramon.

Heidi gained some time by asking Craig for a Corona, wondering what exactly Ramon had heard last night. Had she blabbed to him, too? Or had she done even more than blab? Oh God, this was turning into a nightmare. She wasn't going to have to pay this guy off too, was she? Here she'd been making fun of Katrina for getting so drunk; she was a fine one to talk. Hell, this vacation could turn out to be a lot more expensive than she'd planned.

"She probably wouldn't approve of Pete," said Heidi, accepting her beer from Craig and taking a quick swallow. "Which is why I don't want her to know about him."

"You should watch out for that guy," said Ramon, "he's bad news."

"Oh – and you aren't?" said Heidi with a smirk.

They were interrupted by the return of Katrina, who looked vastly relieved, and had changed out of her sand-soaked bikini and into a cool sundress.

"God, that feels better," said Katrina with a sigh, sipping on her margarita.

"The pee or the freedom from the sand-ass?" asked Heidi.

"Both," said Katrina. "I can sit on a stool now without squirming." She was squirming, in fact – to tell Heidi what she'd overheard in the men's room. But Ramon and Pete were between them, so now was not the time. Pete asked her if she'd like a beer, but Katrina yawned and said, "I think I'll finish off this drink, then it's time for my siesta. I'd kind of like to see part of the beach strip tonight before I pass out."

Pete laughed. "It's done! How about dinner tonight, ladies? Just the three of us," he said, glaring at a beseeching Ramon. "We could meet on the beach and watch the sunset, then go out on the strip."

"Sounds wonderful!" said Katrina, before Heidi could interject. "I haven't really eaten since breakfast."

"Except half a kilo of tortilla chips," snorted Heidi.

"Honestly," said Katrina, glancing down at Pecas by her feet. "I swear the dog ate them all."

Pete and Ramon looked at each other and suppressed a laugh. Ramon said, "Well, it's time for my siesta, too. I have to work tonight selling my hammocks. Not everyone is on vacation here."

He kissed the girls on the cheek, saluted Pete in an ironic way, and wandered off with his hammocks.

Pete, staring after him, said to Katrina and Heidi, "You know, you should watch out for that guy – he's bad news."

"Funny," said Heidi with a laugh. "He said the same thing about you."

16   DINNER FOR THREE

Sunset was spectacular, as promised, and Heidi said, "This is even better than Joe told me." She turned to Pete. "You've got your phone in your pocket. Why don't you give it to me and I'll take a picture of you and Katrina standing in front of the water." She reached for Pete's shirt, and he stepped back with a reproachful shake of his head.

"I don't think so, sweetheart."

"Why not?" said Katrina.

Pete took his phone out of his pocket and held it far from Heidi's reach. "I don't like other people using my phone. Just a little phobia I have."

"Hey!" said Katrina, "That looks just like Heidi's phone."

"Imagine that," said Heidi with a little snort.

Katrina giggled. "I've never seen a man with a pink phone before. Well, not except – "

"Just 'cause my phone's pink doesn't make me a flamer, sweetheart. I like bright colours. Must be the painter in me."

"You paint a lot of houses pink, Pete?" said Heidi.

"C'mon," said Katrina excitedly, "give me your phone, Heidi, I want to take some pictures of the sunset."

"Where's your phone, Kat?"

"The battery's dead, remember? And it's not like I've had time to recharge it."

Heidi sighed. "Sorry, Kat – I left my phone in my cabana."

"How could you!" said Katrina. "You never go anywhere without your phone!"

"Too much tequila, I guess," said Heidi, pretending to be sheepish.

"Well, you might've seen zillions of sunsets from all over the place, Heidi, but I haven't."

Heidi feigned nonchalance. "You've got one gorgeous sunset photo, you've got 'em all."

"I don't know how you can be so blasé about it, no matter how many you've seen," said Katrina. She turned to Pete. "Take some pictures for us, will you? Then you can e-mail them to us or whatever it is you do."

"Sure," said Pete, taking the phone from his pocket. He grinned slyly at Heidi. "Maybe I'll e-mail them to Joe, too."

"Why would you do that?" asked Katrina. "Do you even know Joe? I thought he took off for Puerto Vallarta last night. You weren't even here then – were you?" She gave Pete a curious look; the conversation she'd overheard in the bathroom was still fresh in her memory.

Heidi gave Katrina a curious look of her own, wondering what she was getting at, and motioned to Pete. "C'mon, handsome, why don't you and Katrina go and stand by that palm and I'll get a shot of you with the sunset."

"Oh no," said Pete, "I've got a better idea."

"Oh," sneered Heidi, nodding at the phone. "I supposed you don't want anyone touching your precious instrument."

Katrina giggled and Pete gave a faux leer. God, they're just too cute together, thought Heidi, wanting to vomit.

Pete motioned the girls toward him. "C'mon, girls, we'll take a selfie."

Katrina and Heidi sidled up against him and he put his arm around Katrina's waist. Pete held up the camera and Heidi said, "Give him a little kiss, Katrina, look like you're enjoying yourself."

"Heidi!" exclaimed Katrina, moving away a little.

"Okay, okay, relax," said Heidi. "Just a suggestion."

Pete frowned at her for a second before composing a smile on his face and taking the picture.

"Give me the camera," said Heidi, "I want to see it!"

Pete kept the camera close to his body and turned it so the girls could see.

"Boy," said Heidi, "you really are phobic about that thing."

"If you'd been robbed you'd be a little phobic too," said Pete, putting the camera back in his shirt pocket.

Heidi sighed at the missed opportunity. Obviously she'd have to wait until those two were drunker to get her chance to play photographer. "You know," she said, staring back at the quickly diminishing sun, "this is the perfect time to see the green flash."

"The what?" said Katrina absently, her mind still on Pete's and Ramon's earlier conversation.

"The green flash," said Heidi. "You only see it rarely, if the circumstances are just right. A tiny green flash as the top of the sun touches the ocean. It's amazing."

"That's all bullshit," said Pete, squinting his eyes at the sun, then turning to stare at Katrina, who was just as good a view, if not better. "Someone made up this big story and now everyone in the universe believes it."

"I've seen it," said Heidi, unperturbed. "Twice. Once on the beach in Negril, and once off a catamaran in Zihuat. It was magical."

"Bullshit," repeated Pete. "I was in Zihuat. I didn't see a damn thing."

Heidi watched Pete staring at Katrina and said, "Maybe you weren't looking in the right place."

When the sun had fully set – no green flash tonight — they walked along the main street away from the action, in the other direction, which none of them had seen yet. It consisted mainly of seedy or hurricane-blasted old hotels, then turned into an area of expensive beachside properties.

"Must be nice to have money," said Pete, staring at a particularly gorgeous house nestled among the palms. He glanced pointedly at Heidi, but she looked away.

"C'mon," she said, "Let's go back. I'm starving."

"Oh, come on," said Pete, leading them up a side street. "How much exercise have any of us had today?"

"Too much," said Katrina, shuddering at the memory of her aborted swim.

The girls followed Pete reluctantly, and soon they were met by a sight that made all their jaws drop.

Halfway up the street, they saw a familiar figure. He was on the porch of a nice house, kissing a woman holding a baby in her arms, another small child hugging her leg. He sauntered, whistling, down the path to the road where his car sat, newly washed. His wife and children went inside and closed the door. Pete, Heidi and Katrina approached, and Pete laughed hysterically.

"Ramon! I didn't know the mountains were so close," he said, pounding Ramon on the back.

"Yeah," said Heidi sarcastically, "Why all those bus rides and walking when you've got a car?" She paused. "And a wife. And babies. And here you've been coming on to me. And you're married?"

Ramon glanced back to the house to be sure his family was inside, then stood proudly, as tall as he could.

"My wife is married," he said. "I am not."

133

The restaurant they chose was one of about six along the beach strip, all geared to tourists. They chose this one because it had overhead fans. Even post-sunset, the heat was stifling.

"I thought we came to Pacifico for some real Mexican food," said Katrina, looking over the menu. "This looks pretty gringo to me."

"Oh," said Heidi, "we'll get plenty of real Mexican when we go into town."

"Like Ramon?" said Pete, and they all broke out laughing.

"He's sure a character," said Katrina, looking directly at Pete. "I wonder how he gets enough money for a nice house and a car by just selling hammocks."

Pete caught her look, glanced away and shrugged. "Probably some kind of sideline. You know guys like that – they've always got something going on."

"Do they?" said Katrina, but was interrupted by Heidi, who coughed and said, "Let's order. I'm starting to get faint."

Katrina and Heidi both ordered the chicken mole, on Heidi's advice, with some grilled garlic shrimp to start. Katrina watched in fascination as Pete ordered the grilled lobster and Heidi glared at him. You'd think she was paying for dinner.

"I thought you were kind of broke," said Katrina innocently.

Pete waved a careless hand. "Might as well enjoy while I can." He glanced sidelong at Heidi. "Who knows what tomorrow might bring?"

Pete stared at Katrina. Sure, Heidi was gorgeous, but he'd always had a thing for blondes. And what a blonde! With that long wheat hair, shimmering green eyes, to-die-for body – man, this was one deal he wasn't going to break. He could tell Heidi was getting a bit jealous, too, and he had to laugh to himself. Here he'd slept with her and blackmailed her, and she was still hot for him! Goddamn, this really was the best of both worlds. Two awesome women vying for his attention, and one of them eager to pay for his meal and more. He'd sure be sorry to leave this town.

Katrina was beginning to warm up to Pete – leaning close to him to hear his words, putting a hand on his arm, playing flirtatiously with her hair — and Heidi wasn't liking it much. Okay, maybe she'd set this plan into motion when she was three sheets to the wind, but now that she was half sober, she was regretting it. What if Pete forgot all about her in his conquest of Katrina? Which she was paying for, by the way. Here she was, at the centre of this crazy circus, and she felt like a third wheel.

Katrina's next words made Heidi cringe.

Katrina picked up her mojito to make a toast. "To Pete – for saving my life today."

Pete lowered his eyes and fluttered his long dark lashes like some precocious teenage girl.

135

"Aw," he said, toasting them both. "It was nothing. If I hadn't jumped in, I'm sure someone else would've."

"Yeah," said Heidi, "that mariachi band was just dying to help out."

Katrina gave Pete a kiss on the cheek, but he quickly turned his face so it became a full-on lip-lock. Katrina blushed, but didn't back off. Heidi cursed her phone in Pete's pocket, wishing she could somehow teleport it into her own twitchy fingers. But even if she'd possessed that magic, the moment was soon over. Katrina turned away, cleared her throat, and stared intently at the wine menu. Which, Heidi was aware, she knew absolutely nothing about. Heidi took the menu from her and picked out a bottle of Chilean red.

When the wine arrived, Katrina was happy for a reprieve from the hard stuff. Her head was already starting to spin a little, and she figured that by now she must have more booze than blood in her system. Not to mention that Pete was looking better and better all the time. God, she'd just kissed a total stranger! A tall, dark, handsome stranger! What would Tate think? Oh, who cared, she tried to convince herself. Served him right. She felt more inclined to believe in the psychic right now than in him.

When they'd finished their appetizers, Katrina excused herself to go to the washroom. She looked curiously at the sink between the men's and ladies' rooms, wondering what that was for. She went inside, and rushed back to her table immediately, looking horrified.

"I can't go in there!" she said to Heidi, standing there awkwardly.

"Why not?" said Heidi, "Is there another big bug in there?" She and Pete both laughed, but Katrina didn't join them. "Okay," said Heidi, trying to become solemn. "So is it blocked up or something?"

Katrina leaned closer, not wanting the other diners to overhear. "There's no toilet seat!"

Heidi and Pete laughed harder at this, and Katrina just stared at them.

"I don't see what's so funny."

Heidi controlled her laughter for a moment and said, "There's never any toilet seats in Mexico."

"But there's one in my cabana," insisted Katrina. "There's one in the public washrooms at our pool. So why aren't there any toilet seats here?"

"Who knows?" said Pete. "Maybe they can't afford them. Maybe people steal them."

"Steal toilet seats?" said Katrina in disbelief. She frowned. "What do I do?"

"Well," said Heidi, still trying to control her laughter. "You either go back to your cabana, or – "

"Or what?" demanded Katrina.

"You squat," said Heidi matter-of-factly.

Katrina looked from Heidi to Pete, to see if they were serious. She shook her head in dismay. "Well I sure hope I don't get the runs while I'm down here."

Pete said, "I wouldn't bet on it," and he and Heidi laughed even harder as Katrina strode to the washroom as haughtily as she could.

Heidi caught her breath for a moment and yelled out across the room, "And don't forget to throw the toilet paper in the basket!"

Katrina stiffened for a moment, then hurried to the washroom.

Heidi waited until Katrina was safely inside, then turned to Pete. "Look," she said, "maybe we should call this whole thing off. I think she's starting to like you."

"Wasn't that the whole idea?" said Pete, finishing his margarita and then picking up his wine. "Very nice," he said.

"The wine or Katrina?"

"Both," said Pete, "Look, you're paying me to do a job, and when I do a job, I like to do it well." He paused. "Whatever that entails."

Heidi lost her patience and spoke louder than she'd intended. "Look, I got a little carried away last night – "

The other diners turned to stare in amusement, and Heidi lowered her voice. "How about you just flirt with her a little, make her forget about her boyfriend for a while, then I take a couple of shots of you two necking, you delete those pictures of me on my phone, and we're all good."

"Sorry," said Pete with a shake of his head. "A deal's a deal."

"Oh c'mon," said Heidi, downing some wine and trying to keep her temper under control. "I feel bad now about what I've done, Katrina's too vulnerable right now to deal with your shit."

"My shit?" repeated Pete. "My shit, as you call it, was your idea. And it seems to me Katrina enjoyed that little kiss of ours an awful lot."

"It's not right. Look, you keep the money I gave you so far, I pay for dinner and then you leave her alone."

"How's that going to get you anywhere with Tate?" Pete raised his eyebrows as if in surprise and said, "You're acting almost like you have a conscience. I don't think you're that kind of girl, do you?"

Heidi, furious now, was about to reply when the entrees arrived, followed by Katrina returning from the washroom, commenting on the fact that there were no sinks in there.

"That's what the sink in between is for," said Heidi.

"Oh," said Katrina, and she went back to wash her hands.

Pete devoured his lobster, then excused himself to go to the men's room. Katrina and Heidi were still slowly working on their chicken mole and quickly inhaling the wine.

"I know what's going on," said Katrina out of the blue, and Heidi almost choked.

"I've watched you staring at Pete all night. You want to sleep with him, but Bronwyn told you no more Bad Boys, so you're holding yourself back, and you're getting him to flirt with me so I won't think about Tate." Katrina smiled fondly at Heidi and put her hand over hers. "It's really very sweet of you, Heidi, but – "

Heidi was wondering how on earth to reply to that, feeling even guiltier than she already did, when Pete returned, and leaned over to squeeze Katrina's shoulder. Pete gave Heidi a knowing look, and Katrina gave Heidi a knowing look, and all of these knowing looks suddenly made Heidi's guilt fly out the window.

As Pete sat down Katrina suddenly piped up, "Hey, I have some news!"

Tipsily, she used her finger to lick off the last of the mole sauce from her plate. "That was delicious."

"I told you it was good," said Heidi. "That's news?"

"It's my birthday tomorrow!" said Katrina, raising her wine glass for a toast.

"Holy shit!" said Heidi, raising her glass as well. "I forgot all about it!"

"Everyone did," said Katrina despondently, lowering her glass.

"Heidi told me you had a boyfriend back home," said Pete, sitting down, then grimacing from an under-the-table kick to his leg from Heidi. "Why isn't he here to celebrate with you?"

"It's a long story," said Katrina.

"Very, very long," added Heidi with a roll of her eyes.

Undeterred, Katrina told Pete about the psychic's warning, her problems with Tate and his forgetting about her birthday, and Pete listened, pretending to be fascinated.

As Katrina talked, he put a consoling arm around her shoulder, ignoring Heidi's glare. Finally he said excitedly, "Well don't you see, Katrina? I'm the tall, dark, handsome stranger. I'm the one who causes The Great Upheaval. Why do you care about losing this Tate guy if he didn't even remember your birthday? He sounds like an asshole to me."

"Are you talking about me?" said an angry voice looming above them. They all looked up in astonishment.

It was Tate.

Maureen P. Moore

17 A NEW GUY IN TOWN

After he'd stormed out of the Grub on Thursday night, Tate had gone to a nearby bar on the Danforth and met up with a drinking buddy. After about his fourth beer, he'd considered going back and confronting Katrina. His drinking buddy shook his head sadly.

"Don't do it, bro. Sounds like you're both drunk. Give it a rest, check things out tomorrow."

Tate had resignedly agreed, and his friend, sick of Tate's whining, had changed the topic. "Hey, buddy – what about them Leafs?"

Tate had gone to the men's room a couple of times and called Katrina, but he only got voice mail. Not knowing what to say, he said nothing at all. He wondered what this Great Upheaval shit was all about. Was that why Katrina had been so weird for the last month? And why hadn't she told him anything?

In the wee hours, as he staggered home, he had the brilliant idea of going to Katrina's apartment and facing her head-on. Well, maybe not so brilliant, but what else was he supposed to do? Was she actually going to run off to Mexico tomorrow and ignore the argument they'd had? Katrina had always been so straightforward, but in the last month…

She'd been an emotional ping-pong ball, her feelings all over the place. One day he'd feel smothered by her, the next ignored. She'd call eight times in a day, then not at all. And Tate had no clue why she was acting so crazy. He'd even asked her best friend Cathy at the Grub for some – any! – reason for Katrina's erratic behavior, but all Cathy would say was a tight-lipped "You'll have to ask her."

It had changed the whole tone of their relationship. Katrina had always been the strong, well-adjusted one. Damn, why did he have such a thing for strong women? Maybe because he preferred to float along and let someone else take care of the details of life. Tate knew she was brooding about something, but she wouldn't let him in. He'd momentarily even thought maybe she was seeing someone else, but he just couldn't picture Katrina sneaking around behind his back like that.

And she'd kept babbling on about her 24th birthday, as if it were doomsday. Wasn't it 30 when you started to freak out about stuff like that? But 24??

He'd been unconsciously withdrawing from her, because it wasn't the Katrina Tate knew, shy but happy and easygoing. In fact, before all this birthday shit happened, he'd started to wonder if she was considering backing out; she just didn't seem to take the whole thing seriously, especially when he'd mentioned moving in together.

God, he really couldn't understand women at all. Here he'd thought he knew Katrina – a girl who didn't try to screw with your head or play games. But maybe he'd been wrong about that, too.

A week before the Thursday at the Grub they'd had a fight, and Tate had stormed out of her apartment, saying he thought someone else had taken over her body – or at least her mind – and to call him when she got them back.

So she'd finally called him back for a date – and look what happened.

He'd buzzed Katrina's doorbell a couple of times before looking down and noticing a slip of paper under the door to the salon. He glanced around to make sure no one was looking, then picked up the piece of paper. Definitely Katrina's handwriting, though drunkenly scrawled.

'Kev,' it said, 'Remember our convo last night? Going to Mexico tomorrow with Heidi for a week, town called Pacifico, some place on the beach. Get Marlene to fill in some shifts. Sorry! Make it up to you when I get back. XOXO Kat.'

Tate read the note twice, his eyes swimming, and wondered what to do. Was he supposed to go running after her after the way she'd treated him? And where was this frigging Pacifico place? He'd have to Google it. He'd also have to call his mom for advice; she adored Katrina. But before he did anything, he needed some sleep.

After a long and decidedly accusatory talk with his mom early the following morning, Tate had decided the hell with it, he'd go to Mexico in search of Katrina. The next flight was that afternoon, and he arrived in town with only a vague idea of where Katrina might be staying.

'Some place on the beach,' Katrina's note had said, so Tate had the cab drop him off at the beginning and walked his way down. A place called Joe's Cabanas struck his eye, though it didn't seem much like Kat's style, and he walked up to the bar with his meagre luggage.

As soon as he asked the bartender about a beautiful blonde and redhead, the guy's eyes lit up – as much as they could light up, considering he was quite green and clutching his stomach.

"Oh yeah," said Craig, sweating profusely now. "They're staying here. They said they were going out for dinner along the beach strip somewhere."

"Great," said Tate, looking at the bartender. "Are you okay?"

"Some bad seafood, I think," said Craig, wiping his brow. "Do you want a cabana for the night? Better get it now, 'cause I don't think I'm gonna last much longer. I've gotta call Joe."

"Sure," said Tate, taking a step back, wondering if the guy was contagious. He would've preferred to meet up with Katrina right away, make up and stay with her for the night, but he wasn't sure of Katrina's reception, and he didn't want to be scrounging around for a place to stay at midnight.

The bartender looked at the people around the bar, saw that their drinks were full, then stepped around toward Tate. "I'll get right on it," he said, but suddenly he turned pale, lunged past Tate and ran for the men's room. "In just a minute," he said, dry-heaving all the way.

Maureen P. Moore

18   POOLS AND DRUNKEN FOOLS

Katrina gawked up at Tate. She instinctively removed Pete's arm from her shoulder.

"What are you doing here?" she sputtered, downing the rest of her wine.

"Maybe he's here to celebrate your birthday," said Heidi smugly, "which he obviously forgot before."

"Who's he?" said Tate, ignoring them and glaring at Pete.

"We met this afternoon," said Katrina, "we're friends."

"Wow – fast work for a friend," said Tate.

"Hey," said Pete, rising slightly. "I guess you're the boyfriend."

"Smart, too," said Tate. "Impressive."

Katrina tipsily stood up, not sure whether to be happy that Tate was here, or infuriated. "Are you here to spy on me? Or to apologize for forgetting my birthday?"

"Oh, Christ," said Tate, "Not that again."

"Yes, that again," said Katrina, fuming.

Tate, feeling the tension, decided to lighten things up a little. "Hey," he said as casually as he could, "my mom said she'd kick my butt if I didn't run down here after you."

But that backfired. Katrina scowled at him. "You couldn't even do that on your own, could you? It was all your mommy's idea!"

"C'mon," said Tate. "It was a joke! And I never forgot your birthday, either – that was a joke, too."

"Some joke," said Pete, fully standing now, putting his arm protectively around Katrina. "Do you have any idea of what this poor, beautiful woman has been going through? What's wrong with you?"

"None of your business," said Tate, clenching his fists.

Katrina had never seen him like this, and she had an urge to throw her arms around him. But she was too proud, and too mad.

Heidi watched in fascination. This was even better than she'd hoped for – Tate catching Pete with his arms around Katrina. But Katrina was being overly friendly with Pete and too hostile with Tate. That wasn't in the plan at all. Because she wanted Tate to be jealous of Pete, but she wanted Pete all to herself. And Tate, too. To be honest, she'd probably never see Pete again after this vacation – even though he lived in Toronto, people on vacation always said they'd get together afterward and rarely did. But she'd certainly be seeing Tate – if only he'd just look at her.

"Look, Katrina," Heidi said, "Tate came all the way down here – he obviously cares."

"Or his mommy does," snickered Pete.

Tate looked ready to deliver a blow. The other diners had homed in on the argument and were watching attentively. The waiter, distressed, not wanting a fight, which usually led to a lousy tip, or even worse, an unpaid bill, hurried over.

"A drink, senor?" he asked Tate. And Tate, still glaring at Pete, said, "A tequila. No – make that a double."

As Tate spoke to the waiter and Katrina glared at Tate, Pete let his arm drop from Katrina's shoulder and sat back down. He leaned in close to Heidi and whispered, "Hey, I'd say that guy is pretty pissed off. Looks like you got what you wanted. Why don't you give me the rest of the money and we'll call it a day?"

"It's not enough," hissed Heidi. "Tate's still apt to forgive her once he cools down."

Pete looked closely at Heidi, then shrugged. "Hey, it's your party." He tapped the phone in his pocket and glanced admiringly at Katrina. "I sure as hell don't have a problem with it."

The waiter ran back with Tate's tequila and watched, relieved, as he knocked it back. That might calm things down a little.

But Tate's face was even redder when he turned to Heidi. "You're the one to blame for all this! You're the one who dragged Katrina down here!"

Heidi stood up now, too. "Hey, it wasn't my idea - she just latched on to me, after you rejected her."

Katrina, who'd been standing there watching everyone, still deciding whether to be furious with Tate or not, now turned her anger toward Heidi.

"Latched on?" she repeated, dumbfounded. "I thought you were my friend! I thought you were happy to have me come along, so I could get away from – " She waved her hand at Tate. Then she grabbed Pete's arm and said, "Let's get out of here. I want to celebrate; it's my birthday in an hour."

She glared at Tate and Heidi. "Not that anyone around here remembers – or cares."

Pete stood and smiled and kissed Katrina on the cheek. He said, "No problemo," and grinned snidely at Tate. He looked at Heidi, rolled his eyes in Tate's direction and said, "Have fun," as he followed Katrina out the door.

Heidi flung her hair back angrily and turned to Tate, who was watching their departure, stunned. "Well, that leaves just the two of us," she said, trying to hide the hopeful tone in her voice.

"I don't think so," said Tate with a sneer, and he threw some pesos down on the table and strode out the door.

Heidi slumped down in her chair as she noticed some of the other diners turning away. She felt like yelling "Show's over!" but that just brought a thought of the show between Katrina and Pete that was about to begin – without her and her camera to witness it.

The waiter arrived and placed a billfold in front of her. Heidi stared at it in disbelief. "Well fuck me," she said to herself, as the waiter looked at her, uncomprehending. Heidi shook her head and handed him back the billfold. "What the hell. Mas tequila, por favor!"

Katrina, grabbing Pete by the sleeve, started staggering in the direction of town. Pete stopped her and held her by the arms.

"Look, I know it's your birthday and you want to celebrate, Katrina, but I don't think going into town's such a great idea."

"Why not?" pouted Katrina.

Pete laughed at her, slumping toward him, and said, "Frankly, my dear, I think you're a bit wasted."

Katrina started to protest, and Pete said, "Look, Joe's bar is probably closed, but we could grab some beer or tequila at the store and go hang out by the pool. It's real pretty there at — " He paused, catching himself, and said, "I bet it's real pretty there late at night."

Katrina nodded at the wisdom of his suggestion and hung on hard to his arm as they stumbled down the street.

Tate, totally pissed off at having spent all this money (though in fact his mom had paid his airfare, since she loved Katrina and didn't want to see them break up) and come all this way, figured he might as well enjoy this shithole while he was here – which wouldn't be long, at this rate – and grabbed a cab outside the restaurant and headed toward town.

But he found the surf bars boring, everyone sitting around watching surfing videos, talking amongst themselves about the day's waves, a real clique. The closest Tate had ever come to surfing was lolling around on a boogie board at a friend's cottage. After a drink and a couple of quick shots, he bought some beer and tequila at a local store and took a cab back to Joe's.

Katrina and Pete lay on lounge chairs by the pool, the place to themselves. The only sounds were the occasional hoots of laughter from the cabanas, the usual screeches and howls of night creatures around the grounds, and the breaking waves. Pete sipped from the bottle of tequila he'd bought, and Katrina stuck to beer, sipping slowly, letting out the occasional ladylike burp.

"You're too beautiful for that guy, you know," said Pete, moving his chair closer so he could caress Katrina's arm. "He's obviously a momma's boy. And if he really cared about you, he would've followed you instead of staying back in the restaurant with Heidi."

Katrina frowned. "Oh, he wouldn't stay with Heidi. Those two hate each other."

"Is that so?" said Pete.

"Yes itssso," slurred Katrina, giggling. "She calls him The Slug and he calls her The Princess." Pete was wondering whether to set her straight when Katrina grunted and stared languidly up at the stars. "You know, I never really thought I cared that much about him, until…"

"Until?" prompted Pete.

"Until the psychic," said Katrina.

Oh, here we go, thought Pete. He'd just heard the story, but obviously she was obsessed with it. Though the tall dark handsome stranger part was definitely a bonus for him. He decided it best to change the subject.

"You know, I'd swear you were using me to make your boyfriend jealous back there."

Katrina turned toward Pete, moved closer and dreamily brushed the dark hairs on his forearm. "Maybe," she said coyly, smiling to herself. "But you want to know a secret?" She moved around in her chair a bit, exposing her cleavage to Pete, probably totally unaware of it, but he certainly was. He did his best to stare into her eyes as she said, "I'm not sure if I'm in love with Tate or not – " She giggled. "But I sure like you."

She leaned even closer, still giggling, brushing then grabbing onto Pete's arm, and he thought, all right, now's the time, Heidi or no Heidi. Maybe they could lock lips and he could manage to get a selfie. But as he straightened out of his lounge chair to stroke Katrina's arm, it fell back with a thunk onto the cement, and she softly snored. Shit, thought Pete, talk about a perfect moment wasted.

Maureen P. Moore

19   ROBBERS ON THE RUN

Heidi showed up as Pete was staring at Katrina, trying to figure out what to do with her.

"I see you're sashaying again," he said, slurring a bit.

"Do you blame me, after the way you guys all dumped me at the restaurant?"
She posed provocatively, which was difficult, considering it was hard to stand at all, and tossed her hair. "A couple of the Mexican waiters tried to pick me up."

Pete snorted. "You turistas are all the same – all you want is the local colour."

"That's not what I wanted last night."

"Shhh," said Pete. "She might hear you."

Heidi bent over and squinted down at Katrina. "Did you do it?"

"What do you think?" said Pete.

"Well if you did, you sure wore her out. What the hell did you do to her?"

"Nothing," sneered Pete. "That's the problem."

"Are you kidding?" said Heidi. "It's perfect! Give me the phone!"

Pete looked at the slumbering Katrina and shook his head. "I'm not a goddamn necrophiliac!"

"Christ!" said Heidi, "she's not dead, she's just unconscious."

Pete let out an elaborate sigh. "She looks dead. Jesus, you could send that picture to the cops and they'd lock me up and throw away the key."

"You're being ridiculous," said Heidi. "C'mon, just lie down beside her and give her a kiss – maybe put your hand on her boob."

Pete stood up as straight as he could, trying to be dignified. "No way. I have my principles."

"Oh, right," laughed Heidi. "Like stealing cash but no credit cards. You're a picture of righteousness, Pete."

Her look turned crafty, and she suddenly lunged for the phone in his pocket. Pete swatted her hand away, and she tried with her other hand. Pete took a couple of steps back and would've fallen into the pool if Heidi hadn't stepped forward and grabbed him by the arm. They were both panting when she said, "You know, now that Tate's here we don't have to bother with photos anymore. You can just do a live show."

"Oh," laughed Pete. "So now I not only have to get Katrina into bed, but I have to arrange it so her jerk of a boyfriend just happens to stumble upon us doing it. How do you propose to do that, genius?"

Heidi flung her hair back, trying to look dignified. "I'll figure something out."

"Sure," said Pete, trying to catch his breath. "We don't even know where the guy's staying."

"Could be here for all we know," said Heidi. "This is the cheapest place on the beach, and if I know anything about Tate, it's that he's cheap."

"So — what?" said Pete. "We go knocking on doors in the middle of the night?"

Heidi was about to respond when they heard someone stumbling around the bushes by the entrance to Joe's bar.

"Shit!" cried Pete. "We have to get her out of here! One look at her and they'll think I'm a rapist! Help me get her into her cabana!"

He leaned down unsteadily, and Heidi staggered against him. They nearly fell back onto the lounge chair.

"Okay," said Pete, straightening and taking a couple of deep breaths. "One...two...three..."

They bent down again and lugged on Katrina, who was a dead weight. The noise in the bushes had temporarily ceased, but they knew it could return at any moment.

"You really should stop getting her so drunk," said Pete, breathing hard.

"Me?" said Heidi, huffing and puffing.

They finally managed to get Katrina up to her porch, and they leaned her against the railing as Heidi went through Katrina's purse for the keys. She paused for a moment, and held the purse toward Pete. "Oh, excuse me – maybe you'd be better at this."

Pete growled, and Heidi giggled, found the key, and opened the door with some difficulty – it squeaked as she leaned against it. "Joe really ought to get some WD40 or something for these things."

"I don't think that stuff works on wood," said Pete, moving back toward Katrina and nodding toward Heidi. "C'mon."

They finally managed to get Katrina inside and settled on the bed, after a brief struggle with the mosquito netting. Pete stared down at her. "We should probably undress her – you know, make her more comfortable."

Heidi smacked his arm hard. "You had your chance and you lost it, mister."

They heard a commotion out on the pathway by the pool and peered out the half-open door to see Tate staggering along and bouncing off bushes, carrying a paper bag.

He fumbled with a key, reached a cabana towards the middle of the property, and set the bag down. He struggled with the door a bit, went in, then emerged a minute later in his boxers. He slumped into the porch hammock and opened a beer from the bag. Then he promptly passed out.

"Oh, perfect," snarled Heidi. "We were in exactly the right position with Katrina and you had to go and blow it."

"Look at the guy," said Pete, "he's as bad as his girlfriend. He wouldn't remember even if he'd seen it." He sighed. "It's damn hard to commit blackmail when everybody's passed out all the time."

Heidi looked down at Katrina and sighed. "Well, this night's a bust." She glanced toward Pete with a sexy smile. "But it doesn't have to be."

Pete arched an eyebrow. "What did you have in mind?"

"Why don't we go back to my place and finish up that tequila of yours?"

"Oh shit!" said Pete, "I forgot about the beer and tequila! Someone could have stolen them!"

"How romantic," said Heidi, "that your first thought was of the booze."

"That's not what I – "

"Forget it," said Heidi. "I get the picture. But we'd better be quiet. We don't want to wake up Tate."

"Fifty mariachis couldn't wake that guy up. And I'd think you'd want him to see us together - make him jealous."

Heidi sighed. "Nothing's gonna happen till he gets over Katrina. And that's not gonna happen till he catches her in the act with you." She put her hand on Pete's arm. C'mon, let's go."

They took a last look at Katrina, making sure her head was to the side and there was a waste basket beside it in case she threw up in the middle of the night, then tiptoed out, closing the door as quietly as possible.

They picked up the beer and tequila where Pete had left them, then tiptoed past the snoring Tate. Heidi managed to get the door open to her cabana without too much of a struggle and let Pete in, then closed the door behind him. She took his tequila bottle and downed some. Then she took another gulp but didn't swallow. She pressed her lips against Pete's, prodded his mouth open, and squirted the tequila into it.

Pete, surprised, swallowed the tequila, grinned, and said, "That's kind of weird - but I like it."

Heidi grinned and started undressing. "I've got all kinds of weird – if you want it."

Pete started tugging at his own clothes. "Come to Daddy!" he cried, and they both collapsed onto the bed.

Afterward they dozed for a while, then Heidi awoke, aroused, and snuggled against him. "Let's do it again," she said, stroking his belly.

"Un-uh," said Pete drowsily. "Need sleep." He turned his head toward Heidi with a lustful grin. "I have to save myself for Katrina."

"You don't have to look so excited about it," sniffed Heidi.

"She's not exactly hideous. It's not like I'm dreading the prospect."

"Sure, but she's going to need a lot of softening up. She might be mad as hell at Tate right now, but she still has feelings for him." Heidi giggled. "You're going to have to literally charm the pants off her."

Pete looked at Heidi. "It worked with you."

"Yeah, but I'm easy."

"No kidding."

Heidi sat up, indignant. "You don't seem to have minded too much." She stared up at the ceiling, thinking, then turned back to Pete. "Look, what if we forget the whole thing."

"And forget about my money? No way."

"What if I gave you more money not to sleep with Katrina?"

"And what about your buddy Tate? How're you going to seduce him then?"

Heidi shrugged. "I'll think of something."

"So I'm just your little gigolo, is that it?"

"You've acted like one so far."

"Sure – and you've acted like Katrina's pimp."

Heidi scowled. "You're a jerk."

"And you're a bitch."

Heidi looked Pete in the eye, about to reply, then her eyes shifted to her pink phone sitting on the table beside him. She moved toward him, stretching out an arm, but his hand came down and twisted her wrist.

"Un-uh. Don't even think about it." With his other hand he picked up the phone. Then he released her wrist and climbed off the bed. "I think we're done here for the night."

"Damn right," said Heidi with a scowl. "You're a total asshole-gigolo-petty- thief-Bad Boy. What the hell do I need you for?"

"Besides the phone, you mean?"

Heidi growled and made one more play for the phone, but Pete was too far away. She sprawled out on the bed, seething. "Get the hell out of here!"

Pete found his shirt and threw it on, jamming the phone in the pocket. "You don't have to ask me twice!" He bent over and groped around the floor in the half-dark for his jeans. His fingers touched something cold and metallic, and thinking it was his belt, he picked it up. Only to see his fingers grasping a set of handcuffs.

"Jesus!" he cried. "Is this how you get your men to stick around?"

"Like hell!" Heidi managed to sit up on the bed.

"Your weird just got a whole lot weirder," said Pete, throwing the cuffs on the floor. "Why don't you just stay away from me!"

"No!" yelled Heidi, climbing off the bed. "You stay away from me!"

"With pleasure!" snarled Pete, picking up his jeans.

He started to slip into them when Heidi stepped toward him and gave him a shove. "NOW!"

Pete, one leg in his pants, started to lose his balance, but Heidi pushed him upright, at the same time steering him to the door. He managed to pull his jeans up all the way. He grabbed what was left of the tequila bottle. "Adios, senorita! Hasta manana and all that shit!"

Heidi, fuming, jerked open the door and pushed him out.

He was still trying to zip up his jeans when he stumbled onto her porch, the door slamming behind him with a loud squeak for extra effect.

The yelling, followed by the slamming and squeaking of Heidi's door, woke up Katrina, who'd been out like a log for a couple of hours, but sleeping only fitfully for the last half hour.

Groggy and still drunk, she eased herself out of bed and onto the porch in search of water for her desert-like mouth. As she reached for the glass she kept beside the jug, she glanced across the pool to see the source of the noise that had awakened her. And there, in full view from Heidi's porch light, stood Pete, fumbling awkwardly with the zipper of his jeans with one hand, a tequila bottle in the other. A second later, the window slats were loudly shut and the light turned off. Katrina could no longer see well in the dim light emitted by the pool walkway.

She peered in curiosity as Pete staggered toward another cabana halfway around the pool from hers, looked down at what appeared to be a heap of clothes or a blanket covering the porch's hammock, glanced carefully around, then pushed the door open, somehow without a squeak.

Katrina, figuring that was Pete's cabana, and he was retiring for the night, was about to fill her glass with water from the jug when she saw another figure lunge out of the cabana and race toward the far side of the pool.

Katrina squinted. It looked a bit like that Mexican guy, Ramon, but she couldn't be sure. As she wondered whether Ramon was the thief Joe had been talking about, she was further astonished to see Pete dash out of the cabana and chase after him.

Pete lobbed the tequila bottle after the suspect, but it lurched wildly, landing in the grass beside the outdoor washrooms. He made it a few metres before he stumbled on one of the small lights by the pool, smashing it, and ended up face-down on the pavement. Katrina considered going to help him, but he quickly (with rather rubber-like movements) righted himself, and dashed off in another direction.

If that wasn't Pete's cabana, whose was it? And what on earth was Pete doing there?

This was all too much for Katrina in her current befuddled condition, and she'd just finished filling up her water glass, swigging it down and refilling it, when she glanced back over to the cabana and saw Tate, with all the delicacy of a drugged bulldog, writhe around for a good two minutes, struggling to remove himself from the hammock.

So that was Tate's cabana. What was that all about? Were Pete and Ramon both thieves, in cahoots? Or competing with each other, considering how Pete had chased Ramon? Damn, it was a good thing she hadn't gone to help Pete up, how would that have looked? Then Katrina chastised herself. What was she thinking? Did she care what Tate thought, after the way he'd treated her? Maybe they'd both robbed him, she thought with a snicker.

Then, realizing that Tate would see her if he glanced over, considering her inside lights were on and filtering onto the porch, she quickly scurried inside and shut the door. She certainly wasn't up to talking to him right now. And if he'd followed her all the way down here, he definitely wanted to talk to her. Screw him, she thought. She was drunk, she was tired; she'd see him in the morning.

It wasn't until Katrina set her glass on the bedside table and waded through her mosquito netting that other, more disturbing thoughts occurred to her. She looked down at her clothes. She was still wearing her dress from the night before. Why wasn't she in her nightgown? And there was a wastebasket beside her bed. Where on earth had that come from?

She did a clothes check. Bra still on. Check. Panties still on, dry and in proper order. Check. She suddenly remembered (vaguely) lying on the lounge chair beside Pete by the pool, staring up at the stars. Oh my God, had they done anything?

She checked the bed for signs of evidence. The sheets were unrumpled and dry. Nothing smelled funky. Surely if something had happened there'd be evidence. Unless they'd done it right out in the open by the pool...Oh God!

What if she had done something with Pete? She'd never be able to live with herself. And she'd always been a terrible liar – the guilt would show all over her face – she'd turn beet red every time she even looked at Tate. He'd know instantly.

And if she'd done something with Pete...and then he'd moseyed over to Heidi's cabana after she passed out, to carry on his night? Katrina shivered at the thought. Better to be first choice than sloppy seconds, she supposed, but still...ewww!

20 BIRTHDAY BLUES

Katrina woke up to the squawking of roosters. She'd been hearing them for hours but had always managed to go back to sleep. Now, reluctantly and fuzzily, she sat up in bed, squinting at the bright sun beating through the slats.

Slowly the events from the night before came back to her: dinner with Pete and Heidi, Tate's unexpected arrival, her and Pete at the pool, Pete emerging from Heidi's cabana…

Why, Katrina wondered, had Heidi been urging Katrina to flirt with Pete, when it was now obvious that Heidi was having sex with him? Why? To have first dibs? If Katrina wasn't going to do him, Heidi figured she might as well? What about her Bronwyn/breaking her Bad Boy behaviour rule? Or was Heidi trying to make Katrina jealous for some reason? Maybe to spur her on to flirt more with Pete? But that didn't make sense – Heidi and Pete were obviously hiding this, not flaunting it. She'd watch them together today and see…see what? Maybe nothing had happened between them at all. Maybe Pete just…just what? Fell asleep telling Heidi a bedtime story and just happened to undo his pants, so he'd be more comfy?

Dammit! Yesterday afternoon Heidi was flirting with Ramon, last night she slept with Pete…was she planning on doing every guy in Pacifico or what? Katrina remembered Heidi saying she wanted to get lucky on vacation, but was she going for a world record? After all, she'd only been here two nights. If old Joe was still around, she'd probably be going after him.

The weird thing was, Katrina felt oddly jealous of Heidi being with Pete. Which was crazy – she didn't even know Pete, and he was obviously a Bad Boy, and Katrina was in love with Tate - wasn't she? Tate was the one who should be jealous here, not Katrina!

It was all too much for Katrina's throbbing head. She laid it gently back down on the pillow and dozed off for a while.

When Katrina awoke again, she was momentarily dazed and thought she was back home. She realized it was her birthday, her 24th, and half-expected Tate to come in with flowers and breakfast – things she'd heard other men did for their girlfriends at times like this. But who was she kidding? She was thinking of Tate here – he'd still be sleeping, and she'd never seen him make breakfast in his life.

Katrina came to her senses and jerked her head off the pillow. She'd been dozing, and the sun was slanting harshly into her eyes, and she remembered where she was. Squinting, she thought, what have I done? Obviously, Pete and Heidi had a thing, and there she was last night, using Pete to make Tate jealous. Why had she acted so childishly? She must've really hurt poor Tate, especially after he came all the way down here – even if it was his mommy's idea.

And had something happened between her and Pete? Oh God, she had to know.

She was 24 now, it was time to act like an adult and go after what she really wanted – Tate. No more of this silly jealousy stuff. Or that stupid psychic. Why had she even listened to her, anyway? She was 24, the sky hadn't fallen, and Tate was here, ready to apologize and make up. Tate – the man she at least thought she loved – and didn't want to risk losing.

Katrina, energized now, hopped out of bed, which proved to be a mistake, since that caused her head to swirl and her body to get trapped in the mosquito netting. She was trying to disentangle herself, determined to a) find out if anything had happened last night with Pete and b) go speak earnestly and honestly with Tate, when she glanced through the slats in the window.

And saw, across the pool, Heidi lounging in her teeny-weeny bikini in her hammock, sipping a coffee. And there was Tate, bending over, his face close to hers.

From where Katrina crouched, still enmeshed in the mosquito netting, it looked very suspiciously like a kiss.

When Tate woke up, fuzzy and unsure where he was, he vaguely remembered stumbling back – where? Oh yeah, to the cabana at Joe's. He was here to set things right with Katrina, but she'd snubbed him last night and gone off with that cocky asshole Pete. Had anything happened? Surely his Katrina wouldn't get together with some stranger dude just to make him jealous…would she?

God, he had to talk to her, set things straight. But where the hell was she staying? There were cabanas all over the place here, he realized as he looked out the window. Half of them covered by palm trees. He could go around knocking on doors, or he could go to the office and ask, though they probably wouldn't tell him anyway.

Or he could go look for Heidi.

She was lounging in a hammock not far from his own cabana, in the tiniest bikini he'd ever seen. He felt a little uncomfortable about that, but he took a deep breath and walked up the steps.

"Well, well," said Heidi, sipping her coffee. "Look who's here. Prince Charming, AKA The Slug."

"I'm looking for Katrina," said Tate, forcing a smile. "You must know where she's staying, Princess."

"Sure – in a cabana around here somewhere."

"I'm not in the mood for games, Heidi."

"Me neither. I wish the bar would open. I could sure use a Bloody Caesar."

Tate approached her and leaned close to her ear. "I don't know what kind of shit you're pulling here, Heidi, but if you're trying to screw things up between Katrina and me – "

Heidi laughed. "I think you did that all by yourself."

"So who's this Pete guy?"

Heidi shrugged. "Some roving traveller. We just met him yesterday."

"You work fast – always have, as far as I recall."

Katrina, finally free of the mosquito netting, crouched closer to the window and stared through the slats. No, she hadn't hallucinated in her hungover haze – Tate was still leaning over Heidi in a very intent fashion. She saw movement by the pool, and noticed Pete lying on a lounge chair in swim shorts and sunglasses, a cup of coffee to his lips. Okay, here was her chance to talk to him alone. If Tate kept his eyes locked on Heidi's cleavage, he might not even notice.

And what if he did? The hell with him. The hell with maturity. The jealousy game was back on. Big time.

Katrina grabbed her shorts and tank from Friday's travelling day. They were rumpled and slightly stained, but the only things, aside from the dress she'd worn the night before and her bikini and towel, not wrinkling away in her suitcase. She couldn't believe she still hadn't unpacked. So unlike her. She was usually so neat and tidy. But since Thursday her life had been one big hazy Mardi Gras. She wasn't up to unpacking now, so rumpled and soiled would have to do.

Katrina felt a bit undignified as she staggered out into the brilliant sunshine toward Pete in her grungy clothes, but then she remembered that Pete had seen her only yesterday in her bikini digging at the sand in her butt, and realized she couldn't get less dignified than that.

Heidi, noticing Katrina's arrival, though Tate had been mindlessly staring at her boobs, as if his eyeballs were somehow glued there, pointed with her coffee cup and said, "Looks like you've found your young maiden."

Tate glanced up guiltily. "Uh-oh," said Heidi, 'I think you'd better stand back. You're awfully close, you know." And with that she nudged him aside, stood up, and shoved him off her porch.

Katrina caught a quick glimpse of Heidi nearly tackling Tate, but she huffily ignored them and sat down in the lounge chair next to Pete.

"Hey, gorgeous," said Pete, looking up from some sort of daydream and noticing Katrina for the first time. "Relax and enjoy the sunshine."

Katrina smiled at him and reclined on the chair, but she had a hard time pretending not to notice Tate sprawling down the steps of Heidi's porch. Pete seemed oblivious.

"Hey," he said, looking her over and lifting his sunglasses. "You're not looking bad considering – "

Katrina was about to reply 'Considering what?' and hoping to glean the information she was dying for, when Pete turned his head slightly and she saw the giant shiner on his left eye.

"Oh my God," she gasped, leaning forward, "what happened to you?" though she already knew. Instinctively she placed a tender hand on his swollen eyelid. "Does that hurt?"

"Not when you touch it," said Pete with a wince. "Walked into a door," he said, focusing on his coffee.

"You don't have to lie to me," said Katrina, "I have a pretty good idea what happened."

"You do?"

"Well I don't," said Tate from above them, glaring down.

"Oh, Tate," said Katrina, "how lovely to see you. I was just about to tell Pete how he's my hero."

"Really?"

"Really?" repeated Heidi, emerging on the scene.

"Really," said Katrina, her hand still on Pete's eye, though he looked as if he wanted it desperately to be off.

"Of course. I saw him running after some burglar last night, but then he tripped and fell over that pool light." She gestured toward the broken light. "If it hadn't been for him, God knows what might have happened."

"God knows," said Heidi, rolling her eyes.

"And yesterday," said Katrina, with a sideways glance at Tate, "Pete rescued me from almost drowning."

"I can attest to that," said Heidi. "She was practically lost at sea."

"Your hero," said Tate with a snort.

"My hero," said Katrina, leaning over and planting a kiss on Pete's cheek, then thankfully for Pete finally removing her hand from his swollen eye. "My poor, poor thing."

"Poor thing my ass," said Tate. "I thought there was a guard dog around here. Why didn't he do something?"

"Pecas?" Pete laughed. "He's about as useless as – "

"Maybe the burglar knew him," said Heidi, staring hard at Pete. "And how did you just happen to run into a burglar in the middle of the night?"

"Maybe he staggered into the wrong cabana by mistake," suggested Katrina, not liking Heidi's tone.

"Well, that's certainly possible," said Heidi, tossing her hair in that irritating way of hers. "All the cabanas look the same to me. It's a miracle everyone made it into the right ones."

"Yeah – without everyone falling all over each other," said Katrina with a smirk directed toward Heidi.

"A miracle," said Heidi, looking away at the same time as Pete. "Like I said."

Pete, not liking the direction of this conversation, said, "How about some breakfast, ladies?"

"Don't they do breakfast here?" said Tate, as if accusing Pete of being a bad host. "Where's this Joe guy anyway? It's not as if it's the break of dawn or anything; somebody should be here by now." He glanced toward the bar. "The guy last night was sick as a dog; said Joe was coming back from vacation to cover for him."

"Joe?" gasped Heidi.

"Coming back?" laughed Pete with a glance at Heidi.

Katrina and Tate both gave them a funny look.

"Sure," said Tate. "He's the owner, isn't he?"

"How do you know?" accused Heidi.

"The place is called Joe's Cabanas, isn't it?"

"Oh…" said Heidi. "Right."

"I don't know what shitty kind of place this is," said Tate, "but you'd think they'd at least offer you breakfast."

"It's not the Four Seasons, Tate," said Katrina, suddenly defensive of the place she'd been so horrified of less than two days before and angrily shoving her hands into her shorts pockets. "It's a cheap joint in Mexico, and you get what you pay for."

Tate scowled at Katrina. "Well you'd think you'd at least get a warm welcome."

"You don't get a warm welcome when you barge in. Especially when you treat everybody like crap. Everybody but Heidi, that is."

"What the hell does that – "

"I saw you two on her porch together just now. Very cosy."

"Shit!" said Tate. "I was just trying to find out – "

"Her cup size?"

"No! I was trying to find out which cabana you were in."

"Did you even ask, or were you too busy ogling her breasts?" Katrina avoided looking at anyone and said, "Funny, how Heidi doesn't seem to have any problem booting men off her porch, even though she sure likes letting them in."

She looked up suddenly to see Heidi look sharply at Pete, who avoided her look.

Heidi leaned closer to Katrina. "Now what the hell is that supposed to – "

"Where's that coffee everyone seems to have?" interrupted Katrina, practically leaping out of her lounge chair. "I could use some right about – "

She got no further, because when she'd leapt up so suddenly her hands were still in her shorts pockets, and she lost her balance, falling splat onto Pete's lap. The lounge chair collapsed under them, and the right pocket of Katrina's shorts ripped, and a strip of condoms fell to the ground beside the lounge chair.

Tate, gaping, stared down at Katrina and Pete in their near-coital position for a moment before focusing on the condoms on the ground.

"What the hell is that?"

Katrina, fuzzy from her fall, turned her head as Pete managed to grope around till he found the condoms. He picked them up and read the lettering: "Ribbed. Extra-large. Obviously not meant for you."

Tate rushed forward, ready to throttle Pete, but Katrina was still on top of him, and Heidi managed to push Tate away. Heidi smirked as she said, "A woman has to be prepared." She looked at Pete. "You should probably give those back. At this rate, she might need them."

Pete shrugged and handed the condoms to Katrina, who was trying to climb off of him without scraping her knees on the concrete. She wrapped a hand around the condoms gingerly, as if holding a pissed-off scorpion, and Tate glared at her and shook his head.

"Well..." said Heidi, holding back a laugh, "I'm starving. Anyone else up for breakfast?"

Maureen P. Moore

21   BREAKFAST OF CHAMPIONS

Pete and Tate threw on shorts and t-shirts, Katrina put on a demure sundress, and Heidi simply threw a sarong around the bottom of her bikini. They went to the palapa restaurant on the beach, from which only yesterday Pete had come running to save Katrina from the waves.

Pete selected a table with a view of the ocean, and gestured the girls toward it, making sure Katrina was beside him. Heidi, miffed, sat beside Katrina. Tate was forced to sit next to Heidi, in the only chair facing away from the ocean with a terrific view of the kitchen.

"Sorry, bud, but there's only so many chairs."

"No problem," said Tate, glaring at Pete. "I didn't come here for the view."

Since no one had invited him, and he'd merely trudged along determinedly, not chancing leaving Katrina alone, they all ignored him.

"Think I'll start with a Caesar," said Pete with a grin. "Had a couple of those with my brunch yesterday, before I noticed the lovely Katrina flailing around in the waves."

"Good thing the Great Lifesaver was sober," snorted Tate.

"They have Caesars down here?" said Katrina, acting fascinated as she leaned toward Pete. "In Mexico? I thought they were just a Canadian thing."

Yeah," said Pete, "it's weird. I don't know if it's all the Canadian tourists or what. You can't find clamato juice to save your life in the States, but they sell it in the supermarkets here. Go figure." He stretched and yawned, and both girls couldn't help ogling his muscled arms. "Suits me," he said. "I hate Bloody Marys – too thick; take too long to drink."

"Right about now, that might be a good thing," said Katrina. "I think I'll stick with orange juice, thanks."

"Hey, it's your hangover," laughed Heidi, ordering a Caesar along with Pete.

Tate ordered a coffee, and when the drinks arrived Pete suddenly seemed to remember something and raised his glass.

"A toast!" he said, beaming.

The others lifted their glasses, bewildered.

"To Katrina's birthday!" said Pete, clinking glasses.

"Hey," said Tate, avoiding Pete's glass, "I was supposed to say that."

"First come, first served," said Pete with a smirk.

"What the hell is that supposed to mean?" demanded Tate, half rising from his chair.

Katrina leaned over and kissed Pete on the cheek. "Thank you," she said. "You don't know how much that means to me. Everyone else " — she glared at Tate —"seems to have forgotten."

Heidi rolled her eyes. "Didn't we hear this refrain last night?"

"I told you last night, Kat," said Tate, "I never forgot your birthday; it was a joke." When Katrina wouldn't even look at him, he continued. "I just wanted to get even with you a bit, for making such a big deal out of it. I figured you'd realize I was putting you on eventually. I mean, you used to have a sense of humour. Hell, you just turned twenty-four, it's not like you're an old crone or something."

"You do have a way with words," said Heidi.

"Some joke," muttered Katrina.

Pete said, "So how's it feel to be twenty-four, Katrina?" He waved at the ocean and the azure sky above. "Look, the sky hasn't fallen, no Great Upheaval, no – "

"What the hell are you talking about?" demanded Tate, remembering the girls using those same words at the Grub the other night.

Pete looked at Tate innocently and said, "Surely Katrina told you all about it…you two being so close and all."

Tate glared at Katrina. "You've been telling this jerk stuff you haven't even told me? Sharing stuff with him? What else have you two shared?"

Katrina, feeling momentarily guilty, seeing Tate looking so pained, felt like explaining everything right then and there.

But she still wasn't sure whether she had anything to explain or not. And Pete was not about to lose his advantage.

"We've just been having a wonderful time," said Pete, brushing a long blonde hair off Katrina's face. "You know, like people used to say on their postcards. Having a wonderful time – wish you were here." Pete laughed. "Except, of course – "

Katrina interrupted. "Maybe we should order," she said.

"Tate," Pete said after a moment, with a mischievous look. "You should try the huevos rancheros with chorizo sausages. I had it yesterday. Delicioso! That's what I'm getting."

"That's pretty spicy," warned Heidi, trying not to snicker. She looked directly at Tate. "You sure you're up for it?"

"It's not that hot," insisted Pete. "Just enough spice to get things going, if you know what I mean. Of course, if you're a little too delicate…"

Tate tossed his menu aside and lifted his chin. "Sounds good to me." He turned to Katrina. "What are you going to have? After last night you probably have a sensitive stomach."

"You don't know anything about last night," said Katrina, purposely brushing her hand against Pete's as she put down her menu. "But since I'm not as insecure as you, and don't need to prove my machismo, I'll have the club sandwich, thanks."

Heidi, who'd been busy trying to get the waiter's attention, now turned to Katrina with another suspicious look. Had Pete lied to her? Had he and Katrina done something before she arrived on the scene last night? Had Pete bedded Katrina then decided to go for the daily double and agreed to bed Heidi as well? What was she, sloppy seconds? Ewww!

Katrina saw Heidi's worried look and smiled to herself. If Heidi believed she'd been up to something with Pete last night, maybe Tate would, too. Oh, how she'd love to see him squirm. Katrina had never been a vindictive person, but right now it seemed to go with the territory.

And what was with Pete and Heidi, anyway? Pretending like nothing had happened between them. Was it that feeling-weird-after-sex-with-a-stranger thing? They were pretty much ignoring each other. Was it because Heidi wanted Tate to think Katrina and Pete had hooked up, in a sisterly show of support? Or was she ashamed of going after yet another Bad Boy, after all her therapy with Bronwyn? But at the same time, Heidi was acting almost jealous of Katrina, as if she wanted Pete to herself.

It was all too much for Katrina's throbbing head. She turned to the waiter and asked for a Caesar.

Tate, furious now with Katrina's behaviour toward him, said, "Don't you think you had enough to drink last night?"

"Oh," said Katrina, "you're a fine one to talk. Why don't you go smoke a joint and leave me alone?"

"You like pot?" said Pete, in a new friendly tone. "I can set you up if you want."

"Might not be a bad idea," said Tate, glaring at Katrina. "It's been a while. Some people don't approve."

Pete smiled. "After breakfast, then." He'd only had a couple of small hits off a joint he'd rolled from Ramon's stash, and the stuff was mind-numbing. Wheelchair pot. If Tate hadn't smoked in a while, this might be the perfect way to get rid of him for a while, frying on the beach and drooling up at the sky.

Breakfast started as a silent affair. Tate absently shovelled down his refried beans while Katrina picked apart her sandwich. Pete and Heidi were more interested in their new round of Caesars than the food, and sat sipping and watching the surfers strut by.

At one point Pete turned toward Heidi to make a snide remark about a pseudo-surfer (he was way too nerdy to be a real one) and noticed her staring with open lust at Tate. He glanced quickly at Katrina to see if she'd noticed too, but she was staring moodily at a piece of lettuce on her fork, as if wondering whether it were the e-coli enemy or not. She was oblivious to what was happening a foot in front of her. Pete was not. He wished Katrina would look up, just for a second, but no such luck. The plot was thickening, and Pete always loved the plot to thicken – as long as he wasn't stewing in it too much.

Heidi turned away from Tate and saw Pete staring at her. He winked, as if they were in on something together (well they were, but not this), and Heidi, irritated, decided to make Pete jealous as well as Katrina. She turned in her chair and thrust her breasts toward Tate. "So how do you like Mexico so far?" she asked. Tate looked up from his beans and grunted. "You going to eat the rest of that, or are you just trying to clean out your digestive system?"

Tate narrowed his eyes at her, then plunged his fork into the eggs covered in spicy salsa. "Sure, why not? When in Rome…" He took a huge mouthful, just to spite Heidi, and immediately started to cough. When he could speak again, he waved frantically at the waiter and ordered a beer.

Katrina, watching, snorted, not a very ladylike sound, but it certainly showed her disdain. She moved closer to Pete. "Aren't you hungry?" she asked in a concerned tone, looking at his nearly full plate.

Pete shook his head. "Usually, I get the hangover hungries in a big way, but today…" He batted his long dark lashes and gazed into Katrina's eyes. "Today I'm interested in other things."

Tate glared at Pete, obviously wanting to retort but unable to speak through his cough. He grabbed the beer before it was out of the waiter's hand and chugged half of it down. Heidi, trying very hard not to show her amusement, reached toward the centre of the table and pulled a warm tortilla from an untouched basket.

"Here," she cooed to Tate, "you have to try this. It'll help kill the spice," and she gently rolled the tortilla and fed it into his mouth.

Katrina watched spitefully, then imitated Heidi and took a fresh tortilla from the basket. She rolled it awkwardly and held it toward Pete as she leaned closer toward him. "I know you can handle spice, Petie, but…" and she fed the tortilla into his mouth, though it was difficult considering he had his glass up to his lips at the time. Pete nearly choked, and the waiter, watching and leering from a few feet away, hurried over.

"Ladies," he said with a wide grin, "you need more tortillas?"

Katrina and Heidi waved him away and focused on the men.

Heidi pressed closer to Tate, her cleavage practically rubbing up against him, and ran her tongue against his cheek. Tate started to withdraw, but seeing Katrina's eyes upon him, he leaned closer.

Katrina inched as closely as possible to Pete without sitting in his lap and tongued his cheek as well.

Heidi, watching, was ready to go one step further and started to kiss Tate on the mouth. But he suddenly broke into a sweat and his face turned beet red. His stomach rumbled violently enough for everyone around him to hear, and he stood up quickly enough to topple his chair.

"Toilet," he muttered. Then, more desperately, "TOILET!"

The waiter, sensing his distress, and accustomed to such things from the gringo tourists, tried to hide his smirk as he pointed to the left of the kitchen.

Pete, laughing, grabbed some napkins from the table and shoved them at Tate. "They might not have any toilet paper in there." And they all watched as Tate made a run for the banos.

"I warned him," chuckled Heidi. "The newbies can't take the heat." She turned toward Pete and Katrina and was less than thrilled to see the two of them still scrunched together like Siamese twins. She spoke to Pete with mock concern. "Maybe you should go check on him."

"I think the guy's old enough to wipe his own ass," said Pete. "If you're so worried, why don't you go check on him?"

Katrina wanted to side with Pete and get Heidi to go so she'd have some time alone with him to find out some vital information – i.e., did I sleep with you last night? - but she realized she could hardly get Heidi to stick her head into the men's room. And after Heidi's seduction act with Tate, she wouldn't mind a few choice words with her so-called friend.

"Go check on him," said Katrina firmly to Pete as she leaned away from him and sat back in her chair. It wasn't a question, but a command. Pete studied her for a moment, then shrugged and sauntered toward the bathroom.

Maureen P. Moore

22   ONE MORE DEADBEAT

As soon as Pete was out of hearing distance, Katrina threw a tortilla at Heidi.

"Stop throwing your boobs around," she sneered, "especially at Tate." She glared at Heidi's tiny bikini; the sarong somehow (yeah – right) had come undone and rested on her thighs, exposing most of her body. "And you could try wearing a bigger bikini, or better yet, a one-piece, or – oh, I know! How about a tent!"

Heidi feigned innocence. "Hey, I just thought if I came on a bit to Tate, it would give you the incentive to come on to Pete. Wasn't that the whole idea, after all?"

Katrina stared at her friend coldly. "I think that was your idea."

Heidi sniffed, as if hurt. "It seemed like your idea last night when you took off with Pete and left me stranded at the restaurant."

Katrina leaned closer to Heidi, glanced toward the bathroom to make sure the men were nowhere near, and lowered her voice. "Heidi, I need to know something."

Heidi raised her nose in the air and pretended to be studying the surf.

"Heidi…" Katrina took a deep breath and forged on. "Heidi, do you know if anything happened between Pete and me last night?"

Heidi, stunned, turned away from the ocean and stared at Katrina.

"Now how the hell would I know that? I showed up and you were passed out by the pool beside Pete. He asked me to help you to your bed."

"Well didn't he say anything?" demanded Katrina.

Heidi avoided Katrina's gaze and took a sudden interest in the bottle of hot sauce on the table. "Why would he tell me?"

"Cause I saw him coming out of your cabana last night. So I figured…" Katrina stopped and shrugged, wondering why her friend was being so obstinate.

Heidi looked surprised and concerned for a moment, then regained her aloof look and shrugged. "Like I said – why would he tell me?"

Katrina gaped at Heidi, astonished at her cavalier attitude and just about ready to shake the truth out of her, when a familiar voice came from above.

Well, not too far above, because it was Ramon, who, even standing above them, was hardly a giant palm tree.

He grabbed a nearby chair and plunked himself down.

"How are you lovely ladies enjoying our town?" he asked, undressing them both with his huge brown eyes.

"Where are your hammocks today?" said Heidi.

"Bah!" said Ramon. "It is domingo, I do not work on domingo. It is family day." He frowned down at the beach full of Mexican families, drinking and eating from huge coolers, shading themselves beneath umbrellas.

"Nothing but Mexicans today. They don't buy nothing."

"Ah…" said Heidi. "Family day. "Shouldn't you be with yours?"

Ramon flashed a huge grin. "I would rather be with you beautiful senoritas."

"And your wife and children would rather be with you, I'm sure," said Heidi with a snort of contempt. "If your wife sees you here with us, I'm sure she won't be too happy."

Ramon wriggled uncomfortably in his chair, then looked over the table as if examining a buffet. He homed in on Tate's half-full plate. "Anyone eating that?" he asked, barely waiting for an answer as his hand snaked toward it.

"Not anymore," said Heidi with a snicker, and Katrina couldn't help snickering too.

Ramon pulled the plate toward him and started scarfing down its contents.

"You'd think you were starving," said Heidi, watching him. "You'd never know you owned a nice house and a car."

"In our country, food is not to be wasted," said Ramon with a tiny contemptuous show of his true feelings toward what he considered rich people. Then he seemed to realize the slip in

193

his veneer and grinned broadly, rubbing his belly. "It is far too delicious."

Katrina, feeling mischievous, which was not at all like her, but she considered relevant in the current circumstances, gave Heidi a cursory glance and then leaned toward Ramon. "Tell me, Ramon, are you a Bad Boy?"

"Bad Boy?" said Ramon, insulted enough to stop chewing for a moment. "I am a man, muchacha."

"Sure," said Katrina, "but I bet you've been known to do bad things...especially with the ladies."

"Ah, yes, senorita," said Ramon, puffing up his chest. "I am very bad."

Katrina nodded toward Heidi. "Then watch out for this one. She loves Bad Boys."

Ramon, intrigued, abandoned his now-empty plate, grabbed onto the tortilla basket and changed seats, sidling up to Heidi.

Heidi leaned away and gave him a scornful look. "Isn't there something else you should be doing?"

Ramon smiled, his teeth white against his brown face. He leaned closer as Heidi leaned farther away. "Maybe I will take the day off and spend it with you. You are going to the playa, no?"

"Nice try," said Heidi, finishing off her third Caesar. "Like you said, it's Sunday, domingo, and it is family day in Mexico. You should scoot on home in time to take your wife and

kids to the playa with the rest of your family. Otherwise..."—
Heidi shook her head—"you're in big shit, muchacho."

Ramon was contemplating a comeback when Pete and
Tate returned. Tate was somewhat squinty-eyed, and Pete
grinned like a moron.

"At least you two are having fun," said Ramon, watching
them slump into their seats.

Pete nodded toward Tate. "He's just lucky he didn't
shart himself."

Tate reached into his shirt pocket and pulled out a small
bottle of Pepto Bismol tablets. "I forgot to take these. My mom
warned me." And he popped four tablets into his mouth.

"A little late now for Mommy's advice," scoffed Pete.

"No kidding," laughed Heidi. "You're going to be
bunged up for a week."

Tate ignored her and squinted at Ramon. "Who's this
guy?" he asked, confused. He stared down at where his plate
should have been, thinking he was missing something. Again, he
squinted suspiciously at Ramon. "He wasn't here before, was
he?" He let out a tremendous belch and leaned back smiling,
proud of himself.

"Feeling better?" asked Katrina sarcastically.

"Medicinal marijuana," said Pete." Soothes the belly."

"Shhh!" cautioned Ramon, glancing around the
restaurant. "Don't talk about that around here. You could get us
in trouble."

"Us?" said Pete. "That's funny – you almost make us sound like a team."

Ramon ignored the remark and studied Pete's face closely for the first time. "Hey! Looks like you have a…how do you call it…? A shiner! What happened to you?" Ramon jeered, as he knew quite well what had happened to Pete. Pete's left eye was nearly swollen shut now, giving his stoned face the look of a demented circus freak.

"Just trying to save Joe's from burglars," Pete said, eyeing Ramon. "Thought I heard noises in the dark last night."

"That's weird," giggled Tate, fumbling the tortilla basket away from Ramon and lifting one out, not quite sure what to do with it. "I know I was out of it, but I could swear I heard people yelling and running around." He tried to roll the tortilla but his hands weren't cooperating, so he gave up and began shredding pieces and thrusting them in his mouth. "Starving," he mumbled as he chewed.

"Wonder why," grunted Katrina, rolling her eyes.

Pete gave Ramon a meaningful glance. "I need to talk to you, my friend. I have a sudden interest in buying a hammock." He stood up a little unsteadily and polished off his drink. "Why don't we all meet in about half an hour at the spot where I found you girls yesterday?" He bowed elaborately at Katrina, nearly losing his balance. "Or should I say, rescued you?"

"Rescued?" said Tate, squinting at Pete. "Where have I heard that before?" He stopped, pondering that, then gave up and stared out at the Pacific. "Cool waves, man."

"Oh no!" said Katrina quickly. "I heard there was a calmer beach not far away – why don't we go there?"

"Sure," said Pete smoothly, "that sounds good. Saves me playing lifeguard again. Why don't we all meet at the pool at Joe's? It'll give everyone time to get organized. And we can go swim where we won't be guaranteed to drown."

Pete crookedly pushed in his chair and prepared to leave.

"Hey," said Heidi, "aren't you forgetting something?"

Pete glanced innocently around the table and said, "No, I don't think so." He reached up, felt the sunglasses perched on his head, and pulled them down onto his face. "Nope, everything accounted for."

Heidi knew perfectly well that Pete expected her to pay the bill, as per their 'plan', but she wanted to make him uncomfortable in front of the others.

"The bill," she said, enjoying Pete's look of uncertainty.

"I'm kind of short of money here," said Pete, glaring at Heidi.

Katrina, noting his discomfort, came to his aid. "Pete got robbed in Zipolite," she said, mainly to Tate, as the others already knew.

"Zipper what?" said Tate, squinting at Katrina and rocking slightly in his chair.

"It's okay," said Katrina, reaching for her bag. "We can split it three ways." She looked at the others. "If everyone agrees, that is."

"No, no," muttered Tate, fumbling for his shorts pocket. "I'm having so much fun with all of you, I abso…I really must insist on paying."

Katrina, who knew Tate had always been cheap – though to be fair he had an excuse, he'd never had much money – blurted out, "God, you really are stoned!"

Heidi broke into laughter in spite of herself. Tate continued scrounging in his pockets. "Shit," he mumbled, "I'm sure these are the shorts I was wearing last night. I had my wallet right here." He turned his pockets inside out, showing complete emptiness, aside from a few flakes of lint.

Pete gave Ramon a look, and Ramon shrugged, as if he had no idea what Pete meant.

"Losing your money is one thing," said Pete, glaring at Ramon. "But your I.D. is another story. Pain in the ass to replace that stuff when you're down here. That's what happened to me in Zipolite and I— "

"Zipper what?" said Tate again, squinting at Pete. Then, losing his train of thought, he looked toward the ocean and said, "Awesome beach, man."

"Anyway," said Pete, shooting a look at Ramon, "now I have to wait till I get to Acapulco to get them replaced." He shook his head. "Pain in the ass."

"But why don't you get them sent here?" said Heidi. "You're staying here a week anyway, and I'm sure they have an American Express office or something in town."

"Oh!" said Katrina innocently. "I thought you were taking off in a couple of days."

"What?!" said Heidi, staring at Pete.

"What?!" said Pete, staring at Katrina. "Where'd you get that idea?"

Katrina shrugged as she inspected her nails. "It might've been Ramon who told me."

Ramon coughed and looked away. "Not me, senorita."

Katrina gazed at Pete. "Maybe I mistook you for somebody else."

"That's probably it," said Pete.

"Yeah," snorted Ramon. "All you gringos look alike."

Heidi ignored Ramon and said to Pete, "So you're sticking around, then."

"Of course," said Pete. "But right now I've got to go. Like I said," and he stared threateningly at Ramon, "I want to buy a hammock."

"He doesn't have his hammocks with him today," said Katrina, squinting curiously at Pete, wondering what he was up to.

"Then we'll just have to go to your house, won't we?" said Pete to Ramon.

Ramon, seeing Pete's anger toward him, decided the hell with trying to seduce Heidi. If the guy wanted her all to himself, it was fine with him. Besides, Pete was a lot bigger than him. Ramon had escaped last night, but he might not be so lucky today.

Ramon leapt from his chair, muttered something about family day, and hurried off.

"Hey, what about my hammock?" yelled Pete, and he quickly excused himself and ran after Ramon.

Heidi watched the two men curiously. Tate, oblivious, continued to stare at his pockets, muttering, "Shit, I have no idea what happened here." His face lit up, as if he'd solved the answer to world peace. "But I can go back to my cabana and take a look. My wallet probably just fell out of my pocket."

"Maybe you misplaced it," said Heidi, glaring after a speed-walking Pete. "Happens to me all the time when I'm drunk. I hide my money somewhere that I think is absolute genius, then the next day I can't find it to save my life." She reached into her purse. "I'll pay. I'm already paying for Pete – what's one more deadbeat?"

Tate gave Heidi a stoned, sleepy hug, and for once Katrina didn't really care. She was too busy staring after Pete. She heard a thunk and turned to see Tate sliding off of Heidi, his head landing in the tortilla basket. He was suddenly sound asleep.

"I have to go too," she exclaimed, jumping up. "I really need to use the bathroom in my cabana."

"But all you ate was a club sandwich!" protested Heidi, not wanting to be stuck alone with an unconscious and now snoring Tate.

"Yeah," said Katrina, rubbing her belly as if in pain, "but I don't think I should've eaten that salad. Guess I should've gone for the fries." She threw some pesos on the table, having no idea of their worth, and rushed after Pete and Ramon.

She glanced over her shoulder back at Tate, but decided there was no point in talking to him now, not until she knew if anything had happened between her and Pete. Besides, if she talked to him now, she was pretty sure he wouldn't answer.

At this moment she didn't know if she was mad at Tate or guilty about Pete. But if something had happened with Pete, she couldn't very well be mad at Tate, could she? Tate would be very mad at her. She shivered at the prospect; until this weekend she'd never seen Tate mad before. Damn that psychic! She should be brought up on criminal charges for disturbing the peace!

The waiter came over to clear the table. He looked from Heidi to Tate, shrugged, and slightly lifted Tate's head to remove the tortilla basket. Tate didn't stir; his head simply slumped back on the empty table as he gave a gentle snore. Heidi watched with amusement and a slight revulsion as the waiter threw the leftover tortillas that Tate's tousled hair had just flopped onto into a stack with some others, waiting to be reheated for future guests.

She considered leaving Tate there but was afraid he'd wake up and have no idea where he was. Here she was, with a totally pliable Tate all to herself, and she might as well be sitting with a drunken donkey for all the good he'd do her. For all intents and purposes, she was all alone again, just like last night.

"Well fuck me," she muttered to herself as the waiter brought the bill. She shoved it to the other side of the table and ordered another drink.

23   DUMPSTER DIVING

Katrina ran as fast as she could after Pete and Ramon, despite all the alcohol flowing through her system and the bloating in her belly. She soon was within a few metres of them. Pete and Ramon were on the dusty beach road, and Pete had a death grip around Ramon's quivering neck. Katrina hid behind a palm tree and listened in.

"Look, you little bastard," said Pete, "I want to know what you did with Tate's wallet. Taking a wallet is against my code of ethics. Take the cash, that's all – "

"Yeah, yeah, I heard you at breakfast," gasped Ramon, trying to break away enough to breathe.

"For all that guy Tate knows, it could've been me who took his shit. I'm not about to let you get away with it."

"Screw you!" said Ramon, squirming.

"And screw you!" said Pete, gripping harder.

"Screw you!" said Ramon again, though his voice was getting weaker.

Pete relaxed his grip a little. "Look, this isn't getting us anywhere. I just want to get the guy's wallet and replace it before he realizes what happened."

"What do you care? You got the hots for his girlfriend?"

"Something like that," said Pete. "Now hand it over."

"I don't have it," sputtered Ramon.

"If you spent the cash, I understand, I was going for that myself, but the wallet –"

"No," said Ramon, "I really don't have it!"

"So where the hell is it?"

Ramon sighed deeply and turned his eyes to Pete. "Let me go and I'll show you."

"Yeah, right."

"Honest! It's not so good to stand here on the road like this – anyone could see us."

"Like your wife and kids?" snickered Pete.

"Everybody!" said Ramon. "I have a reputation to protect."

Pete laughed at that, but let go of Ramon's neck. But he kept a firm grip on his arm.

"So show me," he said, out of breath.

The two men stood there gasping. They glanced toward the beach and Katrina quickly hid her head behind the palm tree.

"This way," said Ramon, defeated. "Follow me."

"After you, amigo," said Pete, his hand still firmly on Ramon's arm, though now making it look like a friendly gesture.

Heidi worked on her drink and ordered a coffee for Tate. She was feeling woozy now, but instead of feeling tired, she felt angry. What was Katrina doing, chasing after Pete like some lovelorn heroine? Dammit, she liked Pete, and wanted him to herself, plan or no plan.

The coffee came and Heidi yanked Tate's head off the table. He squinted at her in confusion, and was about to say something, but she raised the coffee cup to his lips.

"Drink up, lover boy," she said fiercely. "I'm not about to drag you all the way back to your cabana."

Katrina followed Pete and Ramon, hiding behind palm trees as best she could. She expected them to end up at Joe's Cabanas, but instead Ramon led Pete just past the place and headed toward a concrete wall bordering the property. They walked along the wall until they arrived at a dumpster. Even from where Katrina stood, squatting behind a giant cactus, the smell was horrific. She tried not to lose her breakfast as she listened in on Pete and Ramon.

"Here, asshole," said Ramon, scowling. "Your precious wallet is right there." He pointed at the dumpster and Pete reeled with the smell.

"You've got to be kidding." He tried breathing through his mouth. Then he shoved Ramon toward it.

Ramon stared at Pete as if he'd gone mad, which he was starting to think might be a distinct possibility.

"So?" said Pete, pushing Ramon closer. "Go on in and get it."

"You crazy, man? I'm not going in that shit."

"You're just lucky that 'shit' hasn't been emptied today."

"I think I'd be luckier if it was," said Ramon, holding his nose.

Pete stared at the dumpster and shook his head, and seeing his chance, Ramon darted off through the empty lot beside them, quick as a gecko.

Pete opened his mouth to shout after him, but realizing it was pointless, sighed loudly, stripped down to his swim shorts, and tied his shirt over his nose like a bandana. He took a deep breath then scrambled over the top of the dumpster.

Katrina emerged from behind the cactus and watched as Pete burrowed in the dumpster. After a couple of minutes and a lot of cursing, he erupted from the dumpster like a man shot out of a cannon, sputtering and shaking his now-filthy hair. He held a gooey-looking wallet in his hand.

"SHIT!" he yelled to no one in particular and began to climb out.

"I hope you got the right one," said Katrina, watching him, arms crossed.

Pete, shocked, jumped from the dumpster, dropped the wallet on the ground, and promptly landed on it. Katrina heard the cracking of plastic. She shoved Pete aside, bent down and picked up the slimy wallet. It was Tate's all right. And all his credit and debit cards were now crushed beyond repair.

She pulled them out delicately and nodded to herself. "At least he'll be able to put the numbers back together."

"What do you care?" asked Pete. "I thought you were mad at the guy."

"He's going to need a ticket to get back home."

"He probably bought a round-trip ticket."

Katrina shook her head. "He probably thought he'd be going home with me." She tucked the pieces of plastic back into the wallet. "I'd better return these to him." She looked at Pete, grubby and grimy from his dumpster diving. "Why'd you go to all the trouble to get it, anyway?"

Pete shrugged. "It's my honourable thief policy. Cash only, no cards."

"Yeah, yeah," said Katrina. "I heard that already. But really – why?"

Pete lowered his head as if ashamed. "I thought you might be upset if you thought I did it – I didn't want you to be mad at me."

Katrina grunted. She felt herself softening – he was awfully attractive, even in his current bedraggled state, shiner and all – but she wasn't sure she could trust him. She focused on hardening her tone. "Who else have you stolen from around here?"

Pete shrugged again. "No one that matters."

"Are you a drug dealer, too?" asked Katrina.

Pete tried but couldn't keep the sarcasm out of his voice. "Oh yeah, babe, I'm the head of a big cartel, that's why I'm staying at Joe's. I'm incognito."

Katrina studied him, unsure of whether he was joking to cover up. Then she looked down at the ground and took a deep breath.

"I need to know something," she said.

Pete watched her clutching on to the wallet.

Katrina looked up at him. "Did anything happen between us last night?"

Pete laughed. "Are you kidding? You were out like a light. Twenty roosters couldn't have woken you up. I don't attack women while they're sleeping."

"You slept with Heidi."

Pete was momentarily taken aback but quickly recovered; there was no point in lying. "She wasn't sleeping, she was drunk."

Katrina laughed feebly. "Oh, so that's different."

"It was her idea," said Pete, holding up his hands in innocence. He gazed at her, batting his thick dark lashes. "I was much more interested in you. But like I said, you weren't exactly available."

Damn, he was charming! thought Katrina, even though he smelled like a rotting carcass and was beginning to fend off flies.

Pete saw her softening and felt his heart go out to her. He did have a heart, though some of his acquaintances might argue otherwise. He felt a sudden urge to protect her.

"Look, Katrina, you might want to keep an eye on your dear friend Heidi."

"I don't know what you're talking about," said Katrina uncertainly.

"Oh, come on," said Pete. "I saw the way she was with Tate at breakfast."

Katrina crossed her arms defensively. "She was just doing that to piss me off a bit. I think she's still kind of annoyed that I joined her on this trip.

Pete snorted. "Yeah, right."

"What's that supposed to mean?"

Pete shook his head and scuffed his sandals against the dirt. "I mean she isn't doing you any favours." Katrina stared at him. He stared right back. "She never did, Katrina, and she never will. Here's a hint: why don't you go spy on her like you just spied on me?"

Katrina's eyes narrowed, and she considered saying something, but Pete just waved his hand in defeat and walked a few feet away to a gate that led into Joe's property.

Katrina watched him in despair. Maybe he was right. Maybe it was time to do some real spying.

Maureen P. Moore

24   HELLO JOE

Katrina was heading back to Joe's through the front entrance, still clutching the stinky and slimy wallet, when Joe hailed her from the bar.

"Hey! Katrina, right?"

Katrina approached the bar and stared blankly at him.

Joe smiled. "You're looking better than the last time I saw you." Katrina remained quizzical. "Friday night. You came in with your girlfriend Heidi. Looked like the trip got the best of you."

Katrina blushed. "Oh – you're Joe."

"I'm usually a little more memorable, but yeah, that's me."

Katrina, still reeling from Pete's words, had a hard time concentrating. "Heidi said you were going to Puerto Vallarta for a week."

Joe looked to the sky, as if seeking salvation. "That was the plan, but my asshole bartender Craig got food poisoning and begged me to come back. The idiot ate some bad shellfish or something." He shook his head. "Been serving seafood here for two years, you'd think he'd know when it smelled bad, wouldn't you?"

Katrina wrinkled her nose. "That's not that appetizer stuff he was serving at the bar, was it – saveechnay or something?"

"Ceviche," said Joe, leaning forward. "God, I hope you didn't have any of it!"

"No, no," said Katrina, her stomach roiling at the thought. "It smelled funny to me. But I wasn't sure if it was supposed to smell like that."

"Hell no!" said Joe, then seeing Katrina's distraught face, said, "You okay? You don't look so good. You want a drink?"

Katrina shook her head. "No thanks. I guess all the booze and strange food are starting to get to me."

Joe clucked sympathetically. "Nothing unusual there. The tourists usually get the runs at some point or other. Just be glad you don't have food poisoning." He rolled his eyes skyward. "That frigging Craig'll get me sued one of these days."

Katrina slumped on a bar stool, suddenly tired and depressed. "You haven't seen Heidi around, have you?"

"Yeah, matter of fact you just missed her. She came stumbling in here a minute ago, had a guy on her arm who looked like he'd just come in from the airport." He laughed lightly. "Kind of like you on Friday, if you don't mind my saying."

Katrina did mind, but she politely said nothing. "Where'd they go?" she asked.

Joe pointed to Heidi's cabana across from Katrina's. "The cabana over there. Think that one's hers. Hard to keep track with all the people coming and going." He paused and opened a beer for himself and held the bottle up to her. "Sure you don't want one?" He glanced at his watch. "Sunday Church is starting in a few minutes; it's going to get busy."

"Church?" Katrina blinked, feeling confused and somehow guilty. She wondered if some strange Mass was about to pop up here amongst the bar stools.

Joe laughed at her expression. "Most of the guests here and the locals who live nearby are usually pretty hungover on Sunday and they can't handle the throngs of screaming, screeching kids on the beach. So I offer up a two-for-one deal for a couple of hours. After that they're sedated enough to deal with it."

Katrina shook her head and Joe looked towards Heidi's cabana. "Strange, the way she came in here just now, no hello, nothin', acting like she didn't even see me. Almost like she was hiding from me. After she was so friendly on Friday night." He held up his hands in mock horror. "I was afraid she was going to come on to me until she latched onto that Pete guy who showed up with Ramon."

"On Friday?" exclaimed Katrina. "Heidi and Pete? Are you sure it wasn't last night?"

"No, it was Friday night, 'cause I drove up to Puerto Vallarta right after I closed up. Heidi and Pete were still here, twisted together like pretzels on their bar stools. I was afraid – "

He broke off as he looked toward the pool.

"Speak of the devil. There's Pete now."

Katrina followed his glance. Pete was standing under the pool shower, shaking his hair like a wet dog.

"Good looking guy, if I say so myself – and I'm not even gay! Don't know about him hanging around that Ramon guy, though – he's bad news."

"Isn't everyone?" said Katrina with a stony look, suddenly sliding off her bar stool. She took a deep breath, clutched Tate's slimy wallet, and strode towards Heidi's cabana without so much as a look or good-bye to Joe.

Joe watched her, then stared down at the dog Pecas at his feet.

"Didn't take her for the rude type," he said, throwing a few tortillas down at the dog. "Very un-Canadian behaviour if you ask me."

25   SPIES AND LIES

Tate, still slightly stoned but on the road to recovery, had followed Heidi up the steps to her porch. There was something he meant to ask her about, but he kept forgetting what it was. And she was acting very strange indeed.

At the sight of the hefty guy behind the bar, Heidi had propped Tate in front of her like a human shield. Whether she was afraid of bullets or recognition, Tate wasn't sure. He had a hard time keeping up as she lugged him toward her cabana and struggled desperately to open the door. Tate's body was lagging behind, but his head was catching up. He followed her inside.

Now that he was coming to his senses, Tate remembered with great embarrassment how Heidi had come on to him at the restaurant, and how he'd been so mad at and suspicious of Katrina that he'd practically gone along with it. God, Katrina must really hate him now. But wasn't Katrina just flirting with that jerk Pete? Shit, he had to pull himself together. He didn't come all the way down here to play stupid games with Katrina – he came here to apologize and get her back.

Tate watched Heidi toss her purse on the table by the door and nervously peer out the front window of the cabana. He wished he'd had another coffee at the restaurant to clear his foggy head. He'd just have to bide his time till his brain cells limped back.

From past experience Tate knew that anger with Heidi wouldn't get him anywhere, so he played it cool. Pretending they hadn't been nearly lip-locked just half an hour ago, Tate casually asked, "So, Heidi - what've you been up to?"

As Heidi turned from the window with a scowl on her face and a sheen on her brow, Tate crossed his arms and said, "Or should I say – Heidi, what are you up to?"

Katrina's earlier intention had been to return Tate's wallet and smashed credit cards, then confront Heidi and find out what Pete had been talking about by the dumpster, how Heidi was no friend of hers. But now that the two were together, she could kill two birds with one coconut. The first thing she needed to find out was why Heidi and Pete had lied to her about being together on Friday night.

She glanced over at Heidi's cabana. What she really wanted to do was stomp over there, break down the door and scream at both of them. But Pete's words returned to her. She'd already spied on him; why not spy on Heidi and Tate, too? It wasn't screaming that was required, it was stealth.

So intent was Katrina on her mission that she barely noticed Pete drying himself off at the pool shower, his back to her as she passed. But as Katrina tiptoed towards Heidi's cabana, Pete turned and spotted her. Surprised by her shiftiness, and realizing she wasn't paying him any attention, he watched her with amusement.

Katrina crept around all the flowery plants and cacti and palm trees. Pete could almost picture her holding a machete and whacking everything down to get a better view. Finally she found a small window that suited her and squatted down beneath it. If Pete didn't know better, he'd think she was having a pee.

"Having fun?" called a coquettish voice, and Pete turned to see a very alluring girl in a barely-there bikini smiling at him. He was intent on watching Katrina, but it would be awfully rude to ignore this beautiful creature. Katrina would just have to spy on her own for a few minutes.

Inside the cabana, Heidi was pretending to be shocked.

"What am I up to? What the hell are you talking about, Tate?"

Tate shook his head with a snort. "Same old Heidi. Always playing games."

Heidi tried to distract Tate by playing the seductress. She almost purred as she stepped closer to him. "But games are fun, Tate. You always loved the games we played."

Katrina was so stunned at what she heard that she stumbled backwards, and her butt landed with a loud crunch on some dry leaves.

Heidi's head spun toward the window. She had to admit she was still twitchy from seeing Joe when she staggered past the bar with Tate. Had Pete e-mailed him the photos of her robbing the bar? Or simply shown him, seeing as he was showering by the pool, in close proximity to Joe? When she'd peered out the window a minute ago, she'd seen Joe talking to Katrina. Heidi had seen Joe nod toward her own cabana and take on an annoyed look. And Katrina had looked downright angry – a very unKatrina-like emotion.

Heidi glanced at Tate and tried to calm herself by muttering, "Damn geckos. They sound like Godzilla when they run through the brush."

But Tate wasn't listening. He'd just remembered the question that had been eluding him. Something he'd heard twice in the past twenty-four hours. "Heidi – what the hell is The Great Upheaval?

It took Katrina a few minutes to rearrange herself. Quietly uprooting herself from dry, crackling leaves and prickly cacti was no easy task. When she finally managed to find her spot beneath the window again, the next words she heard nearly threw her back on her ass.

"Crazy girl," Tate was saying. "How could she fall for that crap? That's just plain idiotic."

"I told you she was an idiot when you first started seeing her, but you wouldn't listen," said Heidi.

Katrina, aghast, poked her head above the window. And saw Tate sitting beside Heidi on the bed, not too close, but damn close enough. Her boobs were pointing at him like missiles, waiting to attack.

"I can't believe this," said Tate, shaking his head.

Heidi moved closer to him. "Would I make up something so ridiculous?"

Tate shook his head again. "I suppose not – but why wouldn't she tell me?"

Heidi shrugged. "Maybe she knew she'd sound stupid. Maybe she thought you'd make fun of her. Or maybe the psychic saying, 'You'll discover who you truly love' scared the hell out of her, made her wonder if she really did love you." Heidi snorted. "As if. You two have always been so casual together."

"Casual..." said Tate slowly. "Yeah, I suppose that's why." His voice sounded a little uncertain. "But still – "

"Or maybe she wanted to check out the tall dark handsome stranger angle." Heidi leaned closer to Tate and put a hand on his arm. "That's probably the real reason she wanted to come here with me."

Tate sat back, frowning, but Heidi continued. "You've seen Pete. He's not exactly ugly. I mean, can you blame her?"

"Heidi!" said Tate, angrily brushing aside her hand.

Heidi wondered if she'd gone too far, but couldn't help herself; when might she get a chance like this again to be so close alone with Tate in private, when he wasn't in a drugged stupor?

"Lighten up, Tate. The way Katrina's been treating you for the last month? The way she's hanging all over Pete now? I mean, who needs it?" She put her hand back on Tate's arm and for a moment he didn't resist. "We were always a better match, the way we used to—"

Tate angrily brushed aside Heidi's hand and stood up. "The way we what? Snuck around and pretended nothing had ever happened between us? And what did you think would happen? I'd tell her about you and then she'd just give me up because you suddenly became her 'friend'?"

Heidi waved Tate's words away. "Katrina's always been a sucker that way. She's too nice for her own good. She would've gotten over it eventually."

Katrina squatted back down for fear they'd see her and thought What on earth? She'd always thought Heidi and Tate didn't even know each other when she and Tate first started seeing each other. And the way they'd always acted toward each other…as if they hated each other's guts. But now…This was unbelievable! Tate and Heidi had both been lying to her! Treating her like a total fool! What on earth was she going to—

Suddenly one of those gigantic flying cockroach thingees flew straight at Katrina's eyes, blinding her. She tried to grab hold of a nearby shrub to keep from falling again, but it cracked under the pressure, sending her down again amongst the leaves and plants. Thankfully the flying freaky thing had disappeared.

Unthankfully, something much worse had shown up instead. As she struggled onto all fours she found herself staring into the eyes of a heavy-lidded prehistoric monster.

Maureen P. Moore

26   SUNDAY CHURCH

Heidi and Tate both jumped off the bed and lunged toward the sounds outside the window, but Heidi got there first. She spotted Katrina, and Tate tried to squeeze around her to get a look, but she shoved him aside with the brute strength he remembered ruefully from past sexual encounters.

Katrina was too frightened to notice them. Wild thoughts flew through her head as she stared at the beast staring back at her. Okay, Wild Animals 101: what were you supposed to do? Don't let them smell your fear. Forget that one; she probably reeked of it. Remain as quiet as you can, even when you want to scream. Well, she was pretty sure her throat was frozen. Don't run, because they're sure to follow. Shit! Forget about that! Katrina sprang up like a kangaroo on crack, tore through the brush and ran.

"What is it?" asked Tate, trying to see past Heidi. "Is someone out there?"

"Of course not," said Heidi. "Just a couple of geckos, like I said before."

Tate tried to move beyond her iron grip. "I don't believe you!"

Heidi watched Katrina leap up and dash off, and then as casually as possible she turned from the window. "Then see for yourself."

Tate eyed her suspiciously, waiting for a trap, but Heidi just shrugged innocently. He edged toward the window and peered through the slats. And saw a retreating Katrina. He was about to yell out to her when Heidi suddenly wrestled him from behind and threw him onto the bed. Tate was so dumbfounded he had no time to react. Heidi reached beneath the bed and her hand emerged with something steely and shiny and not at all welcome. With her other hand on Tate's chest, all Tate could manage was a wheezy "Noooo!" before Heidi latched one handcuff to the bedpost and snapped the other one onto his wrist.

Scratched from the dry leaves and thorny plants and cacti, blood trickling from her legs and face, aware of a strange commotion from the cabana she'd just run away from (were they having sex in there, for God's sake?!), Katrina ran blindly toward the pool. And smack dab into a svelte girl in a tiny bikini.

"Hey!" cried the bikini girl, less irritated by the attack of this Amazon woman than by the sudden severance of her fingers from Pete's beautifully bronzed arm. "There's some kind of monster in there," babbled Katrina, "prehistoric, scales all over it, bulging eyes, hideously awful, and then Tate and Heidi, the cabin shaking, all that noise, and that demon, and – "

The girl forgot her irritation for a moment as she stared at the babbling idiot in front of her. "You mean an *iguana*?" she asked, then broke into fits of laughter.

Pete, unable to help himself, started laughing too. "Guess the spying didn't go so well."

Katrina, now further humiliated, broke into a sob. Then she realized she'd started hugging the girl in some sort of weird shock response and instantly jerked away. But she saw that some blood from her scratched arm had rubbed off on her. Katrina reached to rub it off, but her hand was still holding Tate's slimy, stinky wallet, and it brushed against the girl's skin. The girl jumped back in disgust as Katrina gave up on being polite and dashed toward the street.

"What the hell was that?" shrieked the bikini girl, staring in horror at the blood and grime and wrinkling her nose at the smell, but Pete was already running after Katrina.

"Sorry!" he called after the girl, who put her hands on her hips and scowled before returning her eyes to her befouled arm. Holding it aloft like a foreign appendage, she girlie-ran to the outdoor shower.

"Katrina!" yelled Pete. "Hey, Katrina, I didn't mean to be so…"

But Katrina was already way ahead of him. She may have been a klutz, but she was a good sprinter. Unfortunately, she was sprinting straight for a large throng of partygoers by the bar, all of them chatting and holding plastic cups of cocktails in both hands.

Pete winced and waited for a collision, but the throng parted like the Red Sea as Katrina passed. She even grabbed a cocktail from one of them, like a marathoner accepting a cup of water, chugged it, dropped it, and ran on.

The crowd stared after her and Joe's head whipped from the bleeding and crying Katrina to the pursuing Pete, his shiner prominent.

"Hey!" Joe yelled to Pete, "What the hell did you do to her!"

Ramon, who'd just wandered in from the road and had taken advantage of everyone's distraction to down any cocktails that had been left on the bar, yelled, "What the hell did she do to *you*?"

The crowd laughed, then watched and winced as Katrina reached the road and was nearly run over by a Jeep full of surfers. She sprinted past them just as they braked, and a surfboard escaped, landing with a thwack on the road. The Jeep screeched to a stop and the surfers jumped out and jeered at Katrina and Pete. Katrina ran ahead, but Pete was forced to stop in his tracks at the sight of an oncoming truck. Luckily for him, the surfers had seen the truck too and were too preoccupied with saving their surfboard from certain death to give him the scathing attention he deserved.

The crowd let out a collective breath and was just about to return their attentions to their drinks when Heidi ran up to them, resplendent in her sarong and Chanel bag. She was out of breath and highly agitated, and everyone eagerly parted for her. But just as she was about to exit the property and gain on Katrina and Pete, she too was stopped in her tracks.

The dog Pecas, annoyed by all the new arrivals at the bar (and seeing not a tortilla chip in sight), had sauntered over to the shade by the road and settled down for a nice long siesta. Unfortunately, that came to an abrupt halt when Heidi's foot stomped down on his paw. The normally tranquil Pecas was incensed. He snarled and sank his teeth into the bottom of Heidi's sarong and wouldn't let go to save his life.

Now the crowd and the surfers were all jeering at Heidi, who would have gladly kicked the dog out of her way if not for all the witnesses. An angry mob was starting to surround her when she was saved by the desperate cries of Tate coming from her cabana.

The crowd's ears pricked up and they slowly turned, the surfers joining them. Yes, someone was screaming over there – screaming to be set free. As if on cue, they all stared at each other, then in unison forgot about Heidi and Pecas and ran toward the cabana to see what was up. Their drinks, of course, were still in their hands, though by now somewhat depleted.

Joe got there first and started to turn the door handle. But one of the bar patrons, a real hero, shouted "I'll get it!" and leapt against the heavy wooden door. It squeaked and groaned but didn't budge. Joe shook his head and rolled his eyes and tried to say "It's not lo—" but the hero wasn't listening, and he took a few steps back and barrelled into the door again. "—cked," finished Joe as the blustering fool flung himself through the door, drink in hand, and landed squarely on top of Tate, his rum and coke splashing all over Tate's face. Tate sputtered and bucked and got the guy off of him.

"Hey man!" said the guy, kneeling on the bed and staring at Tate in his handcuffs. "What the hell happened to you?"

By now many in the crowd had crammed into the cabana and were laughing at the sight of Tate handcuffed to the bed. Some broke into whoops and hollers. Ramon stared solemnly down at Tate.

"I told you that one was feisty," he said.

"Oh Christ," said Tate, shaking the rum and coke out of his eyes. "Just get me the damn key. It's on the table there by the door."

Joe parted the crowd and freed Tate. Ramon took the handcuffs and surreptitiously slid them into his pocket. Joe helped Tate off the bed. "How 'bout a drink on me. You look like you could use one."

"Thanks," said Tate, "but I gotta take a raincheck." He elbowed his way through the garish array of Hawaiian shirts and blindingly bright frocks, muttering, "Looks like a frigging luau in here," and rushed out of the cabana, leaving the crowd shrugging and unsure what to do.

"Show's over," said Joe, fearful of losing his Sunday Church liquor sales with all the commotion. He waved an arm. "Back to the bar. Let Sunday Church resume."

Sensing the brilliance of that idea, everyone followed. Tate, running past the bar en route to the beach, was startled at the sight of Heidi wrestling with Pecas. "Serves you right," he laughed, but then, realizing he had no idea where he was headed, he said, "Where'd Katrina go?"

"Not a clue," said Heidi, snarling nearly as much as the dog. "But Pete was running after her."

"Shit!" said Tate, glancing frantically around, then figuring the best bet was probably a bar on the beach.

"No kidding!" said Heidi, now giving up on moving Pecas and working on untying her sarong instead.

Tate ran across the road, Heidi watching with hostility, and the crowd returned to the bar. Joe suddenly remembered his dog's predicament and held his hand up for his customers to wait a moment. He strode toward Heidi and gave her a menacing look. An angry God couldn't have done better.

"I'm not happy about this," he said, glowering. Heidi wasn't sure if he was referring to her robbery of the bar or the injury of the damn dog, but she ignored him and continued trying to untie the knot on her sarong, which had become tighter during her struggles with the dog.

"You're not the only one," snapped Heidi. "I have to get out of here. I have more important things to do than tend to a half-dead dog."

Ramon, who'd followed Joe, replied, "It wouldn't be half-dead if you hadn't half-killed it."

Before Heidi could respond to this strange logic, Joe said, "You'll have to pay for your sins."

"Exactly," said Ramon, folding his arms over his chest in judgment. "Make her pay."

The crowd, listening from the bar where they were eager to get back to Sunday Church, yelled, "Make her pay! Make her pay!"

Joe nodded solemnly and stooped to inspect Pecas's paw. "Hmm," he said solemnly. "Just as I thought." He gently patted the dog and his snarling subsided, but his teeth remained clenched on Heidi's sarong. Joe held up Pecas's bloody paw to show the crowd, and especially Heidi. The crowd roared in disapproval.

Pecas, somewhat mollified by Joe's attention, released his grip on the sarong. Heidi saw her chance and turned to run, but Joe said, "Not so fast, missy."

Joe nodded to Ramon, who happily put a restraining hand on Heidi's arm, uncomfortably close to her breast. Heidi was about to slap the hand away when Joe picked up Pecas and plunked the mangy dog into Heidi's arms. She cried out in disgust. "What the hell!" Heidi tried to turn toward the beach to see where Tate was headed, but Pecas and Ramon were mauling her in equal measure.

"This is ridiculous!" cried Heidi. "I'm not your prisoner!"

"You are until you patch up poor Pecas," said Joe, and he waved Ramon forward. Heidi tried to dig her heels into the hardened sand and ditch the dog, but Pecas dug his claws into her and she screeched. Ramon increased his grip and Heidi tried to jab him in the ribs. He swerved deftly away "Feisty," he grinned as they got close to the crowd. He took the handcuffs from his pocket. "You'd better watch it or I'll have to handcuff you to the bar."

One of the surfers grinned at another and said, "Why haven't we been to this place before?"

"Where do you want the prisoner?" asked Ramon as he guided Heidi through the crowd, which was getting restless. They shouted and held empty cups in the air.

"Just another moment, folks," said Joe. He motioned to Ramon to place Heidi behind the bar, then nodded toward a cupboard. "First aid kit's in there. Pecas can go here." He cleared a spot by the sink and carefully removed the dog from Heidi's scratched arms. She looked ready to run again but Ramon clinked the handcuffs together for emphasis. Once he was certain she wasn't going anywhere – not that there was much room to move behind the bar with the three of them and a dog, anyway –

he reached into the cupboard and retrieved the first aid kit. He placed it in Heidi's hands.

"Now wash that paw real good," said Joe. "We don't want any infections."

"What about me?" sneered Heidi, though she pulled out a cloth and some antibacterial soap. "I probably need a tetanus shot."

"Poor Pecas probably needs a tetanus shot," said Ramon, though he smiled at her lasciviously as he reached for Pecas's paw.

Joe watched to make sure things were going smoothly, then rubbed his hands together and looked up at the waiting crowd.

"Alrighty then. Who's ready for a drink?"

27 BEACH BAR BLUES

Katrina, usually so conscious of what others thought, had barely heeded the din of the bar's 'churchgoers' and the angry surfers, and had sprinted along the beach until the sand slowed her to a jog, then a teary stumble. She looked up and noticed a dilapidated palapa bar not far from where they'd all had breakfast earlier. It sat deserted amidst a sea of Mexican families feasting from their coolers, the children throwing sand and screeching and running amok. No wonder Joe had invented Sunday Church.

Those kids wouldn't be scared of a stupid old iguana. They'd probably catch it and cook it and eat it for breakfast, for all she knew. God, she felt like such an idiot for babbling away at Pete and that girl like that. Of course, she'd been pretty freaked out. But the freak-out over the iguana was nothing compared to the freak-out over Tate and Heidi.

How could they have hidden this from her for so long? Did they really think she was that stupid? Obviously they did, and she was. Why hadn't she noticed? It was just like in a movie, the people who hated each other being secretly in lust. Their words came back to her, and Katrina cringed: Tate saying she was idiotic; Heidi saying she'd always been a sucker. God, she could kick herself.

How long had it been going on? Was it still going on? Had they been seeing each other the whole time she was with Tate? No, impossible: Tate wouldn't do that to her, not the sweet Tate she knew. But then, what had been sweet about him in the past month? All he'd done was ridicule her for rambling on about her birthday and acting a little crazy. Okay, maybe a lot crazy. But she'd had her reasons.

Was it possible Katrina had made Tate into a nice guy in her head just because she needed someone? Because she was in love with him? NO! Definitely not! Not when he'd been loving Heidi all along. The thought of it all was making her sick. And thirsty.

Katrina stumbled over to the little palapa bar, plunked down on a stool and managed to get the attention of the young bartender, who was making out with his girlfriend, long enough to order a beer. She'd forgotten she was still clutching Tate's slimy wallet, and she flung it on the bar when she picked up her beer. Slime! He was nothing but slime. And Heidi, too. God, there was no one to trust around here. That sneaky little Ramon was probably more trustworthy than they were.

Shaking with fury, Katrina sucked back half the bottle of Pacifico in one gulp, then realized she badly had to pee. She tried to get the attention of the bartender, but his lips were locked with his girl's, so she loudly said "Banos por favor!" and he came up for air long enough to motion toward the back of the little bar. There was a little shack there, probably a real shithole, literally,

Katrina thought, and she took a deep breath and staggered on in, quite proud of herself for her mastery of Spanish. And quite displeased to see the lack of a toilet seat again.

Squatting and trying to pee as quickly as possible to avoid the stench – a difficult task while hungover-slash-tipsy – she fumed some more at Tate and Heidi. And Pete! If he'd told her to spy on them – and said that little thing about Heidi not doing her any favours – then that meant he knew, too. And why had Pete and Heidi slept together on Friday and hidden it from her? Was Heidi afraid Katrina would find out and tell Tate, and he wouldn't want to see her anymore?

Heidi had obviously been pissed off when she saw Katrina getting cosy with Pete at breakfast – even though she had started the whole thing by coming on to Tate. So, what were they hiding?

Yesterday Heidi had made it sound like she wanted Katrina to get together with Pete, but then she'd turned around and acted jealous. Did she want Tate *and* Pete to herself? Why had she pushed Pete on Katrina?

And that rat Pete – obviously knowing all about Heidi and Tate and not telling her!

A few metres away on the beach, Pete saw Katrina stumble into the shit shack behind the palapa bar, and stopped in the sand, panting a little. He didn't know how much Katrina had found out about Heidi and Tate, but judging from her mad-dash reaction, it was enough.

And where the hell were Tate and Heidi, anyway? Surely they'd seen and/or heard Katrina crashing through the brush away from Heidi's cabana. Wouldn't Tate want to run after Katrina and try to salvage their relationship? Wouldn't Heidi want to stop him?

Problem was, Katrina, unlike most women Pete had ever been involved with, seemed to be a woman of principles. Knowing that Tate had fooled around with Heidi and hadn't told her would probably mean the end for them. Tate could make up all the excuses in the world and Katrina probably wouldn't listen to him.

So Pete figured he might as well make a last-ditch effort to get it on with Katrina, even though he found himself genuinely liking her – though he wasn't going to let that get in the way of having sex with her. After all, she was broken-hearted and vulnerable, furious with Tate. She just might want some good old revenge sex.

Now that Heidi had been outed with Tate, Heidi might not care anymore – Katrina and Tate were probably kaput anyway – but a deal was a deal, and Pete was determined to get the rest of his money from Heidi, if she didn't want Joe seeing the photos of her. Or better yet, if she didn't want Pete to put them online for the whole world to see. Heidi might not care so much about her boobs being flashed, but that might not fly so well with all of her travel agent clientele – or her family, if she had any. And even if Heidi didn't care about photos of Pete and Katrina making out anymore, Pete would love to show the photos to Tate, just to piss off the golden-haired turd. The way he'd treated sweet Katrina, he deserved it.

Pete approached the bartender and his girl, who were getting back into the swing of things, and said "La senorita?" The bartender looked at him curiously, annoyed by the intrusion. Pete pointed to the shack and the bartender nodded. Pete took the pink phone from his shirt pocket and handed it to the young man. "Fotos por favor?" When the bartender looked blank, Pete added, "De ella y yo." He pointed at his chest and made a clicking motion, hoping the guy would understand his terrible Spanish. He looked befuddled for a moment, and Pete, desperate to be understood, kissed the air. The bartender took a step back, offended, and his girlfriend giggled. Pete hastily threw some pesos on the bar and pointed at the shack again, afraid Katrina might stumble out before he got this arrangement figured out. "Fotos de ella y yo." He pointed at the phone in the man's hand. Finally on the same page, the bartender grabbed the cash and lifted the camera, pretending to take a picture of Pete.

"Like this?" he said, and Pete sighed in relief and slumped onto a bar stool.

"Si, si, just like that. And dos tequila por favor."

The bartender had just finished pouring the shots when Katrina emerged from the back, a disgusted look on her face. She was stepping toward a bar stool when she looked up and saw Pete staring at her.

"Oh, great," she said, "another liar." She started to turn away, then remembered Tate's slimy wallet and reached out for it. But Pete got to it first.

"Sit down and talk to me, Katrina," he said in his most endearing voice. He held up Tate's wallet. "Where else are you going to go?"

"Anywhere but this godforsaken town. Just give me the wallet, Pete, so I can give it back to that a-hole that I used to call a boyfriend. He might need to put the credit card numbers back together so he can report them stolen."

"And why would you help that a-hole, as you call him?"

"So he can go home to his mommy, what else?" Pete released the wallet and Katrina started to turn away.

"C'mon, Kat." Pete took one of the tequila shots and held it to her. "What's the rush? It's not like you can just hop on a plane in the next hour or two."

"Well I sure as hell would like to." Katrina sighed and slumped on the crooked stool next to Pete. She took the tequila from him and downed it, then stared morosely at the pounding ocean. She noticed small children playing in the surf and snorted. "Even they can get in the water without nearly drowning." She looked back at Pete. "You must think I'm a total moron."

Pete grinned. "Well, I kind of thought you were a moron when you ran out on the road and nearly got snuffed out by those surfers."

Katrina snorted again. "Not my finest hour." She glanced sidelong at Pete. "You know, the freakout over the iguana and all."

"Happens to the best of us," said Pete. "I once screamed like a little girl when a gecko found its way into my bed."

"Really?" said Katrina, wondering if he was making that up.

"Cross my heart." Pete motioned to the bartender for two more tequilas. He saw him hand the phone to his girlfriend before reaching for the bottle, but luckily Katrina was staring moodily into his eyes. "Remember last night, by the pool?"

Katrina reddened. "Well...sort of."

"We were having the best time, gazing up at the stars. You were about to kiss me."

"I was?"

"Yeah," said Pete. "Before you passed out."

Katrina reddened even more, and Pete smiled softly. "I wish you hadn't done that."

"Tried to kiss you?"

"No – passed out." Pete leaned closer. "You're beautiful, Katrina. Inside and out. I could tell what you were like, how wonderful you were, from the moment I saw you."

"But I was drowning then."

Pete smiled. "Well…okay. After you recovered. So lovely and kind."

"Oh, Pete." Katrina put a hand on his arm, holding back tears. "If only all of this hadn't happened…"

"Let's pretend it didn't…for now." Pete leaned forward and kissed Katrina, while motioning behind her back at the barman. The barman grabbed the phone from his girlfriend and started clicking away.

"Oh, Pete," managed Katrina, catching her breath.

"Oh, Kat," murmured Pete before putting his tongue into action and glancing sidelong at the phone.

Katrina was starting to reciprocate when something caught the corner of her eye. A flash of pink, glinting off the bartender's manly hand. Something about it didn't gel. She turned slightly and noticed the phone for the first time.

The bartender quickly tried to hide the phone behind his back, but Katrina suddenly lunged at him, grabbing for it. The bartender's girlfriend hissed and looked ready to attack, and he quickly released the phone into Katrina's grip.

Katrina turned to Pete, shoving the phone in his face, sunburn-red with fury. "This is Heidi's phone, isn't it? When you took those photos of us at the beach I should've known you weren't the pink phone type..." She snarled at him. "Being all macho and all."

Pete waved the phone away and backed away a little, fearful Katrina might spit. "Hey, it was Heidi's idea – I didn't want anything to do with it."

"With what?" demanded Katrina, leaning angrily toward him as he tried to lean even farther back, nearly sliding off his barstool.

Pete exhaled loudly then said, "It was all Heidi's plan, honest. It was all that damn tequila she drank Friday night." He motioned the bartender for two more tequilas and accepted his gratefully, knocking it back.

"Of course!" said Katrina, sipping her tequila this time, suddenly feeling the effect. "Of course, a plan! A big, fat, big-boobed plan!"

Pete grimaced. "I gotta tell you, I didn't know you then or I never would've – "

Katrina held up a hand for him to shut up and held on tightly to the phone.

"No excuses. I wouldn't believe you anyway. Just spill it, Bad Boy."

Katrina was reeling, and not just from the booze. She ordered a beer and gulped down half of it, then looked squarely at Pete. "Okay, this is all hellishly awful, but the one thing I don't get is Heidi on the plane saying all that crap about her shrink Bronwyn and no more Bad Boys. And then she turns around and goes right after you! It doesn't make sense. Hell, I wouldn't be surprised if she made it all up."

Pete gave Katrina a knowing look. Katrina almost fell off her bar stool.

"She didn't!"

Pete shrugged. "She saw the name Bronwyn on a sign somewhere and came up with that whole story on the spur of the moment. She was pretty pleased with herself, too."

"But why?"

"She thought if she didn't show much interest in other men, she'd have a chance of getting back together with Tate. You know, since you were acting so weird over the whole Great Upheaval thing."

Katrina shook her head. "Unbelievable." She took a slug of beer, then held the phone toward Pete while still keeping a tight grip on it."Show me the photos."

Pete shook his head sadly. "You really should give the phone back to me, Kat. I need it to get the rest of my money from Heidi."

Katrina held firmly onto the phone. "You'll get it when I'm good and ready. Now show me the photos, and let's start with Heidi."

After leaving a stranded Heidi, Tate had run first to the restaurant where they'd had breakfast and had been snidely asked by a vaguely familiar waiter if he needed to use the banos.

He was still pondering that one when another waiter had sneered, "Maybe another cup of coffee, amigo?" Shit, thought Tate – what the hell had he done in there? With the sound of their snickers at his back, Tate had maneuvered through the piles of beach blankets and bodies and trudged toward another palapa. There he spotted a head of long blond hair. Katrina! But then he spotted Pete beside her, and his blood began to boil.

Katrina had seen the incriminating photos of Heidi robbing Joe's bar, the photos of her boobs, in all their magnificence, and was now looking at the photos of herself making out with Pete. She was just considering whether she should keep them to show to Tate to piss him off, when she felt a shadow looming over her.

"Hey, Pete!" yelled a familiar voice.

Pete glanced up, and Tate's fist rammed into his jaw. Pete toppled off his bar stool and Tate confronted Katrina.

"Nice pictures," he said, nodding at the pink phone still in her hand.

"You should talk. After you and Heidi..." She trailed off, turning away, unable to even look at him.

"You had that stupid no-exes rule!" cried Tate. "How could I?" He took a big breath. "I stopped seeing her just after I started seeing you."

Katrina shook her head in disbelief. "What's that mean? A day...a week...six months?" She downed the rest of the beer and threw some pesos onto the bar. She stood up, taking Heidi's phone and Tate's wallet with her.

"This belongs to you, but I haven't decided whether to give it back to you yet. Right now I'm going to talk to that witch Heidi.|" She strode off, as well as you can stride on sand, nearly tripped over a beach ball, and headed toward Joe's bar.

Tate was staring after her, confused about the whole wallet thing, when Pete emerged from the sand, dusting himself off.

"Didn't take you for the violent type," he said, rubbing his already-swelling jaw.

"I saw the pictures of you two on the phone," said Tate. "What did you expect me to do?"

Pete shrugged. "Relax, nothing happened. If I were you, I'd be worrying about getting my girlfriend back."

Tate had to acknowledge the wisdom of that. He shook his right hand, his knuckles red and raw from hitting Pete. "Shit, what am I going to do now?"

Pete stared at Tate and rolled his eyes. "Go after her, you moron."

28   MORE POOLS AND DRUNKEN FOOLS

Once Heidi had patched up Pecas, the crowd had cheered and now she was a hero of sorts. After all, she had redeemed herself. Joe had rewarded her by buying her a Pina Colada and clearing a stool for her at the bar. But she wasn't quite out of the woods yet, so he'd plunked Pecas on her lap. Heidi had insisted she really had to get going, but Joe said, "So you can run off and handcuff somebody else? Not on my watch."

And Joe had nodded at Ramon, who quickly sidled over to Heidi to keep an eye (and hopefully a hand or two) on her.

Several of the other men, intrigued by Heidi's looks and glamour, not to mention the handcuffs, had quickly moved in on her and clamoured to buy her drinks.

Heidi, caught up in all the adulation, soon forgot about Tate and Pete and Katrina, and glowed in the warmth of hot rum and hotter men.

Katrina, out of breath, ran to Joe's bar and shoved her way through the drunken crowd, not feeling too sober herself. She saw the mane of glorious red hair and made a beeline toward it. Heidi was surrounded by several hunky surfers, a couple of empty glasses in front of her.

"Katrina!" said Heidi in a friendly manner, "I was just going to go looking for you!"

"Yeah, I just bet you were," said Katrina, roughly pushing aside Ramon, who was stuck like glue to Heidi.

Pecas sat on Heidi's lap, happily devouring the tortilla chips she was feeding him.

"I need to talk to you!" declared Katrina, standing as straight and forcefully as she could.

Heidi saw her phone in Katrina's hand and glanced fearfully over at Joe.

"Oh, were you looking for this?" Katrina asked, wiggling the phone at Heidi, but keeping it safely in her grip. "Tell me, why did Pete have your phone?" She knew the answer and thought it fun to see Heidi sweat for a change.

"I uh, ..." Heidi blubbered her words.

"Oh, that's right! I know why." Katrina scrolled through the photos as she held the phone high enough for Ramon to see. "That's an interesting one." She stopped as the topless picture of Heidi appeared. Ramon almost fell off his chair trying to get a closer look. Katrina kept scrolling. "What are these?"

Heidi lunged for the phone, missing and landing in Ramon's grasp. She grimaced and pulled away. While concerned about Joe seeing pictures of her looting his booze, the shots of her flashing worried her more. If Katrina posted them, what would her clients and her parents think?

"Join me and we'll have a chat about those," said Heidi, suddenly sweet as pie again.

"In private," said Katrina, suddenly aware of all the eager onlookers.

"Here's fine," said Heidi, swaying a little, a crooked smile on her lips.

"Okay then!" said Katrina, angry enough not to care about anybody else. "You pimped me out to Pete! You wanted to break up me and Tate!"

"Oh, Katrina," said Heidi with a little laugh. "Don't be so melodramatic."

"And you lied about being with Pete on Friday night," continued Katrina, trying not to hyperventilate. "You pretended you met him on Saturday."

Heidi didn't look the least bit contrite. She petted Pecas and sipped on her Pina Colada. "Hey, I admit I was getting pretty attracted to Pete. I almost went running after him just now until I had a few dog problems. But now that I see there are so many other fish in the sea..." She looked admiringly at the hunky guys surrounding her. "I'm not so sure about Pete anymore."

"I thought you were running after Tate," said Katrina, edging closer.

Heidi laughed, glowing in the interest of everyone around her. "That too. But I'm not so sure he's all that interested anymore, since I handcuffed him to the bed...."

Everyone at the bar hooted and hollered. Katrina stared at Heidi in disbelief.

"You're a real piece of work," she said.

"Thank you," said Heidi, sipping on her Pina Colada. She looked up at Katrina's red, angry face. "Relax, I'm not interested in Tate anymore. I prefer Pete – and other guys." She looked at the men around her.

"How did you dare not tell me about Tate?" said Katrina, seething. "How could you have kept seeing him even after I started seeing him? I thought we were friends. And how could you make such a deal with Pete, trying to set us up so you could tell Tate all about it and ruin things between us?" Katrina leaned in close to Heidi. "You know, it kind of looks like you've just been using me all along."

"Hey," said Heidi, "It's your own fault. I never invited you along on this trip. You jumped on me like a leech and wouldn't let go."

"Tell me one thing," said Katrina. "Why did you even fall for Tate in the first place? He's no Bad Boy."

Heidi shrugged. "He used to be – when I fell for him two years ago."

"TWO YEARS?" cried Katrina in astonishment. "You were seeing him for TWO YEARS and I didn't know?"

Heidi laughed. "No, just for a couple of months before you met him. I was just pining for him before that – he was with that stupid Iris chick. Then I thought, great, he finally broke up with her, and then you had to step into the picture."

Heidi petted Pecas "I thought you had him for sure, until your Great Upheaval bullshit. You got so clingy then, and seriously, you were a mess, a giant pain in the ass, so I thought I had my chance. And then when he showed up here, and I'd already laid the groundwork for you and Pete to get together – perfection! Only I didn't count on Pete actually having morals, or you having balls, or Tate actually caring so much."

Heidi sighed. "So unfortunately, I think you and Tate actually deserve each other, and Pete ended up liking you more than I'd planned on, and I ended up liking him more than I'd planned on." She shook her hair in distress. "Pete's having morals has kind of spoiled him for me. I was really starting to fall for him – he made me so mad all the time."

Katrina put her face right up to Heidi's. "Pete doesn't have that many morals. He planned to take off as soon as he finished with me. He wasn't going to tell you. After he got his money, he was just going to leave. I heard him telling Ramon that in the bathroom by the pool."

Ramon, still close by, looked worried. But Heidi, instead of being upset by this, seemed happy. "He was really going to do that?"

Katrina nodded. "He sure was."

Heidi grinned. "Well! I'm having second thoughts about him now."

Katrina scowled. "Well I'm not having second thoughts about you." She held up her hands, as if to fight. "I'd like to knock you out right now, but I refuse to hit a woman who has a dog in her lap." She suddenly lurched toward Heidi, who cringed backward on her stool, nearly falling over. Pecas squealed and dug his claws into her. Heidi screamed.

Katrina suddenly knelt down and grabbed Heidi's big purse from beneath her stool.

"Hey, that's Chanel! What the hell are you – " Heidi gasped, and Katrina threw the bag with all her might toward the pool. It landed in the deep end and quickly sank.

"That's Chanel!" repeated Heidi. "That's premium leather!" She jumped up, Pecas forgotten, and forced her way through her admirers and toward the pool. Katrina slowly followed her, an amused smile on her face.

Tate and Pete arrived on the scene, faces flushed, breathing hard. They were blocked by the shouting crowd, which was now facing the pool, fascinated. Tate jumped up to see over their heads, and quickly shoved his way through, Pete following.

Heidi jumped into the pool, emerged, spluttering a bit, then she took a deep breath and dove into the deep end.

Katrina turned for a second and saw Tate and Pete running toward her. She held Tate's wallet tauntingly in front of him, then swivelled and launched that into the deep end as well.

"Hey!" cried Tate. "That's my wallet!" He dove into the pool, narrowly missing Heidi, who shot out of the water with her Chanel bag in her hand.

Pete, seeing the bag, yelled, "Hey, my money's in there!" and he, too, dove into the water. He collided with Heidi, who was struggling to swim one-handed with her precious bag. She tried to keep it away from Pete, and they struggled, sputtering and going under again. Tate emerged from the pool, wallet-less, and heaved in great gulps of air. Never a strong swimmer, he latched onto Pete for support. They all struggled to stay afloat, with about as much dignity and hissing as drowning cats.

Katrina, watching all this with a smile, now broke into a grin, and then a laugh, and she slowly clapped her hands. "Wonderful!" she said. "I think the three of you absolutely deserve each other!" And she turned on her heel and strode straight to Joe's bar.

Maureen P. Moore

29 THE GREAT UPHEAVAL NO MORE

Katrina managed to get a flight out the next day. It cost way more than she'd hoped, but she would've paid twice as much to get away from that hot mess.

After she'd left the pool, she'd motioned to Joe, who was momentarily free, since all his patrons seemed to have drifted to the pool area to watch the Heidi, Pete and Tate show. Katrina first showed him the pics of Heidi robbing his liquor cabinet.

"Shit," said Joe, "I thought my count was a little low, but I just thought Craig must have been partying with some friends. And he was so sick from the bad seafood that I didn't have the heart to confront him. Guess I'll have to have a little talk with that girl." He nodded toward the pool. "If she ever gets out of there."

Before Katrina could stop him, he scrolled over to the photo of Heidi flashing her boobs. "Wow, nice tits...er, boobs," said Joe, glancing sheepishly at Katrina. He looked thoughtful. "You know, I might have to be a little more lenient with her than I thought."

Katrina sighed and asked him if he knew anywhere she could stay for the night - no offence, but she really had to get the hell out of there. He recommended a place a friend of his owned in town, made a call for her, and she quickly packed - not difficult, since she'd really never unpacked.

As Katrina shifted in her economy middle seat, squirming to make it even a tiny bit bearable, a man in his forties made himself comfortable in the aisle seat beside her.

"Alex," the man extended a hand to Katrina.

"Katrina," she replied as she shook. She couldn't help but notice he was tall, dark, and handsome.

"The kids are sad to be heading home," he told her. "My wife and kids are up in first class. It's a thing we do on the return flights. They get time with Mom in the big seats. Virginia used to hate flying home – now she looks forward to it."

"I take it the kids aren't little ones."

Alex laughed. "No, that would be far from relaxing for her. Alex Jr. is twelve and Brandon is ten. They can keep themselves occupied."

Katrina nodded.

"What about you? Are you sad to be leaving paradise?"

Katrina laughed. "Beauty is in the eye of the beholder. My eyes were certainly opened on this trip, but I'm very happy to be leaving – the place and the people I came with."

Boarding had completed and the plane backed away from the gate.

"I don't mean to pry," Alex said, "but I'm all ears if you want to talk about it. It's kind of what I do."

Katrina wasn't sure what that meant, but she suddenly felt her eyes pooling with tears. After all she'd been through the last few days - not to mention the last month - it would be good to talk to an impartial party. She took a deep breath and began her tale of woe.

Katrina spent the next thirty minutes spilling her guts, fortunately not literally, to her seat mate. Alex was a good listener, occasionally asking a clarifying question but not interrupting or making any judgement.

"So there you have it – the story of the Great Upheaval."

"It's an interesting story," he replied. "Your parents should be very proud of the way they raised you."

Katrina looked at him, confused on how the recent shit show would impress her folks.

"Let me explain," he replied, seeing the confusion on her face. "One of the greatest challenges in life is to be true to yourself. As they say, you need to love yourself before you can truly love another. I think you have found your true love – yourself."

Katrina sat there, stunned.

"What's the name of your hair salon?"

"Kat's Kuts."

"Around the corner from the Danforth, right?"

"You know it?"

"Yes, my office is on the Danforth." He reached into his pocket, pulled out his wallet, and handed her a business card.

She read it out loud. "Alex Bronwyn, Psychologist, Danforth Ave., Toronto."

Katrina's mouth hung open. Everything that kooky psychic had said had come true: She'd met her tall, dark handsome stranger, and discovered who she truly loved.

THE END

A SMALL FAVOUR

I hope you enjoyed Beach Bar Blues. Can I ask a small favour?

Leaving a review helps authors, especially independent authors like me!

I appreciate every honest review of my work. It only takes a few minutes – it doesn't need to be an eloquent composition, just a few thoughts will help incredibly! Posting to Amazon or any book site would be appreciated.

Thanks for your time!

Maureen P. Moore

Trials of Katrina Series

Amateur Sleuth / Romantic Comedy

Maureen P. Moore

Dale J. Moore

Dale J. Moore

These books can be read as standalone stories, or consecutively.

Book 1: Life of the Party

Maureen P. Moore

'Outgoing? Gorgeous? Enjoy P/T evening work? Good fun! Good pay! THIS IS PERFECTLY LEGAL!' The ad in the Toronto paper sounds just about perfect for Katrina. Except for the 'outgoing' part. Desperate to escape a creepy roommate and a scary landlord, she must find some way to supplement her meager café salary to flee to a new apartment.

Eye-popping beautiful but woefully shy, when Katrina is hired as a professional guest (aka PEST) for a company called Life of the Party, her nerves get the best of her. Before she can make a total fool of herself and lose her new job, she's saved by a dashing and mysterious stranger who vanishes into the night.

With the help of her newfound friend and fellow PEST Cathy, Katrina tries desperately to find her mystery man. Her search, and her life, gets disrupted by the nefarious affairs of her roommates, landlord, and new boss. Along the way, Katrina learns that she may be shy - but she's certainly no wallflower.

"Moving to the city was incredibly intimidating, but being able to come home every night and read about Katrina and her adventures brought us immense joy during the transition."
Anonymous reviewer

Book 2: Friends of the Deceased

Dale J. Moore

How does a small town girl end up investigating crime at a funeral home in Toronto? Drop-dead gorgeous Katrina is trying to run her new salon and take her relationship to a new level. The unexpected death of a client and struggles with her salon lead her to the Shady Rest funeral home.

As she stumbles her way through the personal problems that plague her world, Katrina ends up immersed in the world of preparing people for the next world.

With the help of a ruggedly handsome police detective, some old friends, and a few new ones, will she get to the bottom of what's going on, or end up buried by it? One thing is certain; when Katrina gets involved, chaos and comedy will ensue.

"Behind-the-scenes hijinks at a funeral home will have you cheering for hairdresser Katrina and her gang when they delve into stolen goods, fraud, and charity scams. Katrina has to unravel the mysteries before the next ultra luxury casket is made for her."
Nancy J. Cohen, Author of the Bad Hair Day mystery series

Book 3: Days of Wine and Tomatoes

Dale J. Moore

Katrina is back for her third chaotic adventure! Trying to revive a struggling relationship with her detective boyfriend, they're off for a long weekend to wine country along the shores of Lake Erie. Customary to Katrina's exploits, trouble crosses her path like a black cat, altering the idyllic getaway. As the town of Leamington holds its annual Tomato Fest, the summer waterfront party atmosphere is disrupted by a kidnapping. Mixing the enjoyment of the lake front wineries with sleuthing and rooting out clues, Katrina missteps from one mishap to another while solving mysteries in her unique way. Having been the Life of the Party, and after surviving Friends of the Deceased, Katrina's latest escapade has barrels of wine and laughs. Mix in a bushel of tomatoes, a misfit crew, and the summer sun, and you've got Days of Wine and Tomatoes.